Donia Kamal is an Egyptian novelist and producer. She duced more than fifty documentary films and numerous t shows for various Arab networks. She currently lives between Egypt and the UAE, working as a senior producer for the Middle East broadcasting network Al Hurra TV, interactive shows mainly focused on current events anc *Seven* is her second novel.

Nariman Youssef is a translator a ily in Arabic and English. Her tran fiction, poetry, song lyrics, and the controversial constitution draft. She serves as translation manager at the British Library for a digital archive launched in 2014. Having grown up in Cairo, Nariman has lived and worked between Egypt and the UK since 2001. She holds a master's degree in translation studies from the University of Edinburgh.

Cigarette Number Seven

Donia Kamal

Translated by

Nariman Youssef

First published in 2018 by
Hoopoe
113 Sharia Kasr el Aini, Cairo, Egypt
420 Fifth Avenue, New York, 10018
www.hoopoefiction.com

Hoopoe is an imprint of the American University in Cairo Press
www.aucpress.com

First published in Arabic in 2012 as *Sijara sabi'a* by Dar Merit

Published by arrangement with Dar Merit

The poem extracts in this book are from: Amal Donqol, "al-Mawt fi lawhat" (p. 96); Amal Donqol, "al-Buka' bayna yaday zarqa' al-yamama" (p. 97); Salah Abdel Sabour, "Qasidat ahlam al-faris" (p. 109); and Mahmoud Darwish, "Mawt akhar . . . wa uhibbik" (p. 172). All translations are by Nariman Youssef.

Exclusive distribution outside Egypt and North America by I.B.Tauris & Co Ltd., 6 Salem Road, London, W4 2BU

Dar el Kutub No. 26268/16
ISBN 978 977 416 850 5

Dar el Kutub Cataloging-in-Publication Data

Kamal, Donia
Cigarette Number Seven / Donia Kamal.—Cairo: The American University in Cairo Press, 2018.
p. cm.
ISBN 978 977 416 850 5
1. Arabic Fiction
892.73

1 2 3 4 5 22 21 20 19 18

Designed by Adam el-Sehemy
Printed in the United States of America

Nothing lies between us and happiness
but the demons that lie within us.
—Naguib Mahfouz

Dedication

I LIKE INTRODUCTIONS BUT DON'T really know how to write them. Maybe by my next novel I will have developed the ability to craft the kind of opening that draws the reader in. But for now, let me stick to a few words of dedication.

To "the demigods" and to the violin player whose music travels to me across communication channels—you are not like the others, so stay as you are!

To the faces I lost track of, the faces I tried to keep, and the faces that hurried past me but left a lasting impact. To the moments we spend lifetimes trying to capture. To the child who has not yet read my words, and to the promised day when she will. To my family by birth, and to my other family by choice. To the friend who chose to leave but is still—I'm certain of this—watching over me from afar. To good company, to allies, and to the small, colorful places that bring together our troubles and reluctant joys.

Finally, to the one who keeps the promise of a more innocent world alive.

1

I SAT NEXT TO MY grandmother on an old wooden couch in the spacious apartment and watched as she sifted uncooked rice to remove the small stones and mites that might have crept into the cloth sack she had bought at the cooperative. On a bed in the same room, my grandfather lay on his side next to the radio. The voice of Umm Kulthum was interspersed with radio static. For the rest of my life I would never learn to appreciate Umm Kulthum without the static.

I was not yet five years old, and had been living with my grandparents for as long as I could remember. My grandparents lived on the fifth floor of a huge, ancient building on the main road of a small city. There was no elevator, and Grandma often carried me up the wide staircase. I didn't talk much, but I absorbed every detail around me: every grain of rice on the red tray on Grandma's lap, every word in the song coming out of the radio—"the evening sauntered toward us, then harked to the love in our eyes"—and every line on Grandpa's serene face as he listened.

Grandpa gestured, calling me over to him, and, still lying on his side, took me in his arms and rocked me in time with the music. The joy on his face in that moment is stored deep within my memory. But so is the way his face suddenly contorted and his arms slackened around my small body. I also remember how Grandma jumped to her feet and rushed over to us, and that he tried to reassure us both.

I wasn't a child who cried. I didn't cry when Grandma closed Grandpa's eyes, calmly carried me into bed next to him, and pulled the covers over the three of us. Nor did I cry the following morning, when men and women in dark and ugly clothes came to console my grandmother, who wasn't crying either. My grandfather's illness had eaten away at his liver and killed him. The only time I cried was when Grandma switched the radio from Umm Kulthum to the Quran. By the time my mother arrived from the Gulf, also in black and tearfully mourning her father, I had stopped crying.

Grandma wore black from the day of Grandpa's death until her own, fifteen years later. Her spacious home was filled with sadness. I would look at the photograph of my grandparents on the wall, then at Anwar Wagdy and Layla Murad on TV, and feel confused—I couldn't tell them apart. Although, as contradictory as it may sound, my grandmother resembled both Layla Murad and Amina Rizq. She was Layla Murad with her big smile and her gravity-defying hairstyle, but she was also Amina Rizq with her sternness and strength and the handkerchief wound tightly around her head.

Grandma rarely took me out. All I knew of the world was the rusty black radio, the books that she brought to teach me to read, and Grandpa's room at the end of the apartment, where I wasn't allowed on my own because she said it was full of ghosts—and there *was* something ghostly and magical about that room with the old wooden TV that was always covered in a white bedsheet. I knew nothing about the outside world. My mother said that when she started to take me out, I would stand in front of streetlamps and ask their names, and that whenever she switched on the TV I would enter into long monologues with news anchors and stomp my feet when they didn't reply. All I knew about the world came from my grandfather's laughing face and the songs of his beloved Umm Kulthum.

He talked
And I talked
Until we finished all the words

2

I ABSORBED DETAILS. I REMEMBER my mother, sitting with her sister in my grandfather's room, and me in the middle, as if I weren't there. They were discussing things—people; maybe relatives. Were they talking about the men in their lives, their marriages? Maybe. They talked, and sometimes they cried. Then Grandma came in and silently, gently, led me to the other room. She dressed me in going-out clothes—a nice pink and blue summer shirt and blue cotton shorts. My hair was long and dark. She combed it, somewhat roughly, and put two flower hair clips in it, one on each side. I sensed drops of water on my head and looked up at my grandmother, but her face was unchanged except for the tears she quickly wiped away.

She took me by the hand to the photographer's studio and told me to smile: he was going to take my picture but first he had to see my teeth in a wide smile. I tried and tried. Finally my features cracked into a tight little smile that more than anything conveyed suspicion. I didn't show my teeth.

3

UMM KULTHUM SANG AGAIN, AFTER months of Quran on the radio, months in which the only color I saw was black. My grandmother moved with her big rice tray to the kitchen, abandoning her wooden couch, and naturally I moved with her. I watched her and hardly spoke. Everything she did was slow and deliberate.

Coffee brewed on the small stove. She brought onions and garlic cloves in from the small kitchen balcony, and slowly and skillfully peeled the garlic and sliced the onions. When my eyes started to water, she ordered me out of the kitchen, but I stubbornly refused. She layered the onion and garlic along with sliced potatoes in an elegant oven dish, whose colors fascinated me, and placed it in the oven. Then she coated the chicken with flour, vinegar, and salt, and placed a saucepan filled with water on the stove. When bubbles started to appear on the surface, I told her the water was boiling. She smiled—the world's tightest smile—and dropped the chicken into the water, just for a few minutes, before taking it out and placing it on top of the potatoes in the oven. To do that she took out the oven dish with her bare hands, without using a towel. My grandmother's fingers were old and crinkled, so maybe her nerves had died, or maybe she enjoyed the pain of heat on her aged fingers.

When she was done with the potato dish, now a chicken-and-potato dish, she placed the copper pad, which prevented food from scorching, on the burner. She put a saucepan on top of it, put in some ghee and semolina, and sprinkled in a few drops of mastic. She added wet rice to the mix, which sizzled and immediately released its delicious aroma.

I sat on a chair, resting my cheek on my hand and looking at the ceiling, ready for the awaited moment. My grandmother looked at me, her tight smile slowly spreading across her face. "You're dying for a coffee, aren't you?" she said, and I turned to her eagerly. She got up and placed the coffeepot on the burner. When it was ready, she poured most of it into a big white cup for herself and a few drops into a tiny porcelain cup—which must have been part of a toy set—for me. Yes, I was a child who drank coffee. A five-year-old in a big kitchen in front of a red tray full of rice, sipping coffee and waiting for the moment that always came and made everything look wonderful: I would look up and see that all the colors had deepened. The potato dish was reddish gold now, the chicken on top almost done. The rice was in the pot and the plates were set before us.

4

I HELD ON TO MY father's hand. We were in a vast, beautiful park that had a big pond, in which snow-white birds swam. I wasn't interested in jumping around like the other children. My sole ambition was to get as close as possible to the ducks and geese in the pond. I pulled at his hand and he laughed. "What is it you want, my girl? You want to feed the geese? OK, OK, easy now!" We went to the park caretaker, who gave me some breadcrumbs to throw to the birds in the pond. But I wanted to put the bread in the geese's mouths. My father laughed. He held my waist so that my upper half was dangling toward a goose, who snatched the piece of bread out of my small fingers. I frowned for a moment, and then threw myself into my father's arms.

Then he took me to get ice cream. We sat together at a metal table. I smeared my face with ice cream while my father read the newspaper, occasionally peering at me from behind its pages and his glasses. "Having fun?" he asked with a big smile. I nodded, content, then climbed off my chair and went over to dirty his face with an ice cream kiss.

5

Life in our apartment in Madinat Nasr started when I was barely seven. I had only been a few months old when my mother left me with my grandmother and went to the Gulf. We didn't own a house and my father didn't have a steady income, so my mother bent over backward to get a job overseas. She took my sister with her and left me behind. My father objected, but when my mother set her mind on something, nothing could stop her. For the next few years, my grandmother took care of me and my grandfather, who was sick. I remember the black radio and my grandmother's delicate finger pressing the play button, the bowl of mashed vegetables she would be trying to get me to eat held in her other hand. That play button was the only thing that coaxed me into eating. Umm Kulthum's deep voice succeeded where all other grownup games failed to overcome my childish stubbornness. Her voice and the words she sang—"How could they possibly remind me? As if I would ever forget!"—even outshone the funny faces my sick grandfather would pull to get me to open my mouth.

Later on, when my father took me to live with him in our new apartment, he came up with another strategy: stories that ended only when my plate was cleared. Tales of fantastical animals, giant gateways into magical worlds, colorful creatures on planets in faraway galaxies, stories about children—"Once upon a time there was a boy called Galal and a girl called Galila." My storyteller father made up tales of animals who rebelled against the kings and laws of the jungle, and he didn't give up until I opened my mouth for the spoon.

When my father took me from my grandmother and I started going to a school in Heliopolis, I began to experience feelings of estrangement, something they say all children, who are living mostly inside their own private worlds, occasionally feel. I really hated school. I hated studying and I hated all the teachers and nuns; I couldn't stand the classes and all the words and numbers they made us learn. I think it must have been around that time that I developed my fierce stare and my steely armor began to form. I became known for being antagonistic. I spoke very little and was constantly being compared to my cousins, who were of course friendly and sweet. "I don't know why she can't be more like the other girls in the family," my mother would say, with an underlying bitterness, to anyone who was listening.

At school, there was this annual charity event and everyone would be in a frenzy preparing for it for weeks. Donations were collected and kids from several orphanages were invited to spend "a lovely day" at our school. Girls from neighboring schools would come to help. Everyone was supposed to get involved. The teachers prescribed poems and speeches that we had to learn and recite for our orphaned brothers and sisters, in the presence of the district director of education. I would spend that day every year hiding in the small enclosure between the playground and the nuns' residence. No one ever went there except for the dada, the taciturn school nurse. I would sit on the lawn with the skirt of my school uniform gathered between my legs and a book on my lap. The dada often saw me and placed a finger on her lips to reassure me that she wouldn't tell, and I would pass the day reading and dozing on the grass, until the noise of the other kids told me that the school day was coming to an end. Then I would gather my things and join them.

6

He leaned on my arm as we marched in the direction of the square. I could hear him struggling to breathe but I urged him on anyway. We needed to keep up with the other marchers and escape the state security men who were scattered everywhere. We kept walking at moderate speed. My friends were at the front, but I couldn't go to them because I didn't want to let go of his arm. He whispered to me, "Is this the revolution then? Am I really going to witness a revolution before I die?"

"It looks like it could be. Just tell me if you're tired, and I'll take you home and come back."

"Are you kidding? Fifty years I've waited for this day. I'm not going anywhere and you're staying with me!"

He smiled and I smiled back as we walked on along the downtown streets that were leading us to where the battle was.

Demonstrations filled the streets of Cairo. No one could have predicted the turnout. Around us were faces of all colors, of all ages and classes. There were young women with colored veils framing their angry and determined faces, and others with uncovered hair swinging behind them as they chanted in high voices that I couldn't help but chuckle at. I was too embarrassed to join in the chants. My thin voice wouldn't convince anyone. I thought I'd leave the chants to the rough voices of men, and held on to my father's hand.

"Where did all these people come from?" he whispered again.

"Apparently from Facebook," I answered, unsure. "Look, Baba, I don't know, but they're here. I just hope it ends well."

"Of course it will, silly!" He seemed confident now. "If anything was ever going to end well, it's this."

I gave him a look full of doubt.

We kept on walking through the narrow streets. The numbers increased as we neared the Ministry of Interior. I didn't want to go there. There would certainly be trouble. In a calm tone, as if I weren't really scared, I said, "Why don't we go grab a coffee somewhere until things calm down a bit?"

"Really?" He looked at me sharply. "You want to leave all this? For a *coffee*? And you know I don't drink coffee because of my blood pressure."

The chants picked up around us. I had to shout for him to hear me: "Have tea then! Anise tea or something. Let's just go have a drink!"

"Listen!" he snapped back. "I want to go on. If I get tired, I'll tell you. Then we can rest somewhere."

I surrendered to the flow of the march that was now certainly leading us to the Ministry of Interior. My heartbeat quickened, with fear but also with an inexpressible joy. I was in a demonstration along with thousands of people, and I was walking by my father's side.

7

Years ago my father took me to Talaat Harb Square during a small protest. There was a man with very white hair, and a man who was being carried on the shoulders of another and leading the chants. I remember that day well, and that the lead chanter's voice held more bitterness than zeal. His chants were directed against specific names. My father held my small hand in his and held his other hand up with the victory sign. He had tears in his eyes. There weren't that many protestors that day: twenty, or maybe thirty. They stood on the sidewalk outside Madbouli's Bookstore. The white-haired man was trying to stir people up; he spoke ardently and angrily. Within minutes the riot police were there: seven or eight lines of them surrounded the small group. Things started to get tense. My father held my hand tightly. "Scared?"

"Of what?" I answered boldly. "I'm never scared, you know that."

"Just so you know, it's OK to be scared," he said. "You just don't need to be scared when I'm with you."

I clung to his arm. "I said I'm not scared."

"Why don't we leave now? Let's go get an ice cream at Groppi, then go home."

"But I don't want to leave!" I said stubbornly. "Please, let's stay a bit longer."

"OK, but only fifteen minutes, then we have to go—before the beating starts."

He was firm about this. I didn't get it at the time. What beating? And why? I didn't see anything that called for a beating. The man chanting made me sad, for a reason I didn't quite understand. He himself seemed sad. His voice was hoarse from all the chanting, but still loud. I imagined myself in his place, carried on someone's shoulders, my thin voice convincing no one. The names they repeated in their chants must have been those of bad people, or, as my father put it, "bastards." My father's foul language used to make me blush. Only years later did I realize that his language was not foul enough to describe those bad people.

That day, we waited until my father—the omniscient god in my small world—sensed that the beating was about to start. He dragged me toward Groppi Café.

We sat at one of the old and rusty metal tables. People were gathering by the windows and the door, whispering to each other as they tried to see what was happening outside. My father ordered a mastic ice cream for me and a medium-sweet coffee for himself. I was not scared. I was ten years old. Nothing scared me, and I had my father's hand to hold on to. How could I be scared then? My father did not look out the window; he knew exactly what was happening outside. Every now and then we would see someone run toward one of the surrounding buildings. We heard muffled noises. My heart sank. Cautiously, I asked, "Baba, has the beating started?"

"Yes, but don't be scared. No one is going to harm us."

"I told you I'm *not* scared." I hit the table with my open palm. "I just want to know who's beating who. And what they did."

He answered, "Well, sweetie, the policemen outside are beating the people who were yelling. And the people who were yelling don't like that there are bad guys in our country. And they also don't like that when they say that the bad guys are bad guys, they get a beating."

I found all this very strange. "But why don't they call the police? The police would handle the bad guys."

He looked at me with something close to pity. "Didn't you see the policemen outside? They're the ones doing the beating. They work for the bad guys. It's ugly, I know. The people outside want to change all those ugly things."

I frowned, beginning to sense the gravity of the situation. The bad guys were vile and the police were vile. The people outside were getting a beating because there weren't many of them. I reached this conclusion as I got ice cream all over my face at Groppi and a small battle raged outside. I wasn't scared; I had my father's hand.

We left and got into our blue Fiat 128 and drove over the big bridge, my father talking the whole way. Sometimes I got confused: was he talking to me or, as was more often the case, to himself? He was talking about prison.

"In the sixties, when I was arrested during the big crackdown, we were taken to al-Wahat, a very big prison near the Western Desert oases. It was rough. We were beaten often. I'll show you the scar I still have on my leg when we get home. They sometimes used a whip, which wasn't even the worst thing. Everyone was beaten, left and right."

I later understood he meant the political left and right.

"We couldn't stand each other, but I felt sorry for them. I felt sorry for myself too." The next car veered too close and jammed us up against the sidewalk. "You call that driving, you moron!"

I listened, swaying between apprehension, fascination, and anger. I imagined a big room where one of the bad guys made the good guys line up on both sides—left and right, as my father had said—and gave them a beating with the whip, which in my mind was a thick red hose, not unlike the one we had in our bathroom and which my mother often put to similar use when I did something she didn't like.

"Baba, keep going. Then what?"

He was still looking at the other car in the rearview mirror. "Well, not much. They kept moving us from one prison to another. It was shit. But you know what? Somehow those were good days. I wrote a lot in prison—stories that I still have. I had all my friends there with me, and I made new friends I still have to this day. I mean, if it wasn't prison and we weren't being beaten up, I would have wished those days would never come to an end."

I listened to my father and tried to understand what he was saying about prison, about torture, about friendship. I wondered if he and I could be taken to prison by the police I had seen earlier, and if, once there, we would relive the magical stories he was telling me. The thought filled me with fear and awe. But my father had a weak heart now. He wouldn't be able to withstand a beating from the red hose. I, on the other hand, was used to the hose and could take anything.

Take me, you brutes, and leave my father!

8

The first time I met Ali, we were in a large, crowded coffeehouse. Someone was talking incessantly at me so I was too distracted to give Ali's eyes the attention I immediately understood they deserved. I captured the moment and saved it: Ali's eyes were to be my discovery of the year. The coffeehouse was crowded and loud. I hate crowds and I hate noise, so I wasn't relaxed. I stole a few curious glances at Ali, but we didn't talk that day.

The next time I saw him was at my place. There were fourteen of us, in a space that could barely fit four, for the sunset meal one joyful Ramadan evening. Some mutual friends brought Ali along, and finally I met him properly. His irises were one solid color—I still don't know how to describe his eyes, except that they seemed to me like windows onto the world.

I could never understand the dazzling look in Ali's eyes. Did he see an unspoiled world? Did he see these damaged people as children, discovering the world for the first time, touching everything with their curious fingers? Did he look up at a clear sky? Was the world for him like Alice's Wonderland? Did he see trees in brilliant greens and yellows with blossoms that reached the limits of color? Did he see colorful birds and white doves flying in peace, out of the hunter's reach? Did he see us as we really were, underneath the smoke and smog and petty things that killed the sparkle in our eyes? Were our eyes—the eyes of those of us who were damaged by blood and defeat and unfinished revolutions—innocent and pure to him as well?

How did he see the world and us? How did his eyes carry so much innocence and wonder and peace?

The strange thing was that whether he smiled, laughed, or frowned, there were no lines around his eyes. They stayed calm and clear, nothing disturbing the innocence that emanated from them. When his gaze escaped into faraway meditations or memories, or even to painful thoughts, the same look remained, the same clarity that was like a soft wave caressing a sandless beach.

In one lucid moment, which I carefully captured and preserved, I knew I was going to fall in love with Ali, that my destiny would be tied to his. I woke up a few days later to find his hand clutching my wrist. He was clinging to my hand in his sleep, his breathing close to my face. Love was fearful at first, reluctant, drawing near for a moment before disappearing for days—I could see it and not see it. But time passed beautifully. The doubts came and went.

When I looked out of the big window in my apartment, Ali would come up close behind me and put his arms around me; he held me tightly and rested his head on my shoulder, and time stood still.

Not all my moments with Ali could be captured. It was an incomplete happiness. But when he looked at me, my heart skipped a beat. When I received him at the door of my small apartment I was embraced by the universe. I was miserable when he left, but every time he returned, he brought whole galaxies with him. Ali was everything I wanted to see every time I opened my eyes. Ali was the path I would follow until I closed my eyes for the last time and crossed over to another world.

9

I ONLY LIKE TO WALK on the beach. I don't like swimming in the sea—all the salt water and jellyfish and mysterious creatures and dangerous currents. No, I don't like swimming in the sea at all. I don't really like walking either. Lying on the sofa has always been my ultimate pleasure. But I do like walking by any body of water.

In my early teens, I used to walk by the canal near my grandmother's house. It would be cold, the streets nearly empty. Canal water is dark, without the beauty of the sea. I would walk and walk until I got to the base of the big statue where I sat down to count the passing ships. They were giant oil tankers. I could smell their cargo as I counted them and watched those who came and went around me: men, women, young people, strolling as people do by the water. Children played by the base of the statue, but I barely heard the noise they made.

I got that feeling whenever I found myself surrounded by water. I imagined myself floating on its heavy surface, and sometimes I imagined myself surrendering to its depths.

I dreamed about death a lot, though I wasn't really sure if they were dreams or visions. I saw myself dead in a variety of clichéd ways: I opened the door of a speeding car and rolled on the asphalt until blood poured out of my body. I walked on the narrow ledge of the balcony, my back to the building's cement wall. Then, calmly, without any of the fuss of jumping, I let my feet slip into the air. I stuck the kitchen knife into my wrist. A fountain of blood gushed out. I saw myself dying all the time. Death was the only dream that stayed with me. An overdose of sleeping pills. A rope around my neck. And I was always fully present, executing my death with skill.

Sitting under that impressive statue by the canal, I couldn't have known that, many eventful years later, I would become even more adept at these thoughts. I couldn't have known that, as I sat chain-smoking and contemplating the ceiling in my small studio—the smallest apartment in the world—I would still be at exactly the same spot.

My studio was almost unlit, tiny. It had no rooms. Just a few meters of space, a small sofa bed, two lamps that gave off a faint yellow light, a big comfortable sleep-inviting armchair, and a "wailing wall"—the large bathroom that was perfectly suited for locking oneself in to cry. Many people visited that place: friends and work colleagues. Dozens of friends and friends of friends used to stay over, in complex sleeping arrangements.

*

The first time my father came to visit, I cleaned the apartment and prepared a feast.

For two days I stood in the kitchen, making all his favorite dishes. I made rice with semolina, boiled in chicken broth, the way he liked it. The chicken was well marinated with all kinds of spices, except black pepper, which he was allergic to. I put a large onion in a clay pot, added carrots, peas, zucchini, and potatoes, drizzled everything with olive oil, and placed the pot in the oven until the vegetables were crisp and golden. All were relatively low-fat dishes that wouldn't give him atheroma or threaten his weak heart. I cut the salad into big chunks—my father believed that small-cut vegetables lost their health benefits. He also liked mint leaves in his salad. I made fresh orange juice. I prepared everything. I compiled a playlist on my new laptop of songs by Abd al-Wahhab—his favorite musician—and waited for him.

While we ate, my father told me the story of how he met my mother. Whenever I teased him that it was a mistake, he would reply, laughing, that it was the mistake that gave me life.

With a smile full of nostalgia he began to speak:

"I was in Germany. I went there after the 1967 defeat, once I had been released from prison, and had written a book about all the traumas in my life. I left wanting nothing more to do with Egypt and lived like a drifter, working one day out of ten. At night I cried because I couldn't go back. I missed Nasser's funeral and, like all the other exiles, cried as I watched it on TV. Then one day, I found out from a friend that the novel I had written was finally being published in Egypt. I asked several friends to buy copies and keep them for me in case it sold out. Among those I asked was my niece, who wasted no time and went straight to the Cairo Book Fair. What I didn't know then was that she had taken a friend from university along. They were young, early twenties, while I was well into my forties. A few days later, a week or so, I got a letter from Egypt. It was from a young woman, your cousin's friend, who later became your mother, saying that she had read my book, was in love with me, and wanted to marry me. I was spellbound. I thought she must be hideous, with protruding teeth or something, or pretty but stupid. But still, I couldn't resist. I replied, and we wrote to each other for over a year. She sent me her photo. She was so beautiful, much more beautiful than I could have imagined. And she was intelligent too."

"So you fell in love with her?"

"Of course. I loved her very much, even before I met her. She was the fairy tale in my life—it was a story that could only happen in a novel. That in itself was enough for me to love her. I came back, we met, we got on with our lives, and we got married."

"I have no idea how Grandma agreed to it, Baba."

After a long laugh, he said, "Your grandmother was a powerful woman, but your mother even more so. When I went to propose, your grandmother told me, 'Listen, son, you are a poor man, a piecemeal journalist, you don't own an apartment, you're always on the move between countries, so you're not the settling type, and you're more than twenty years older than my daughter, and—no offense intended—you have a criminal record. Let's just say that I have no daughters available for marriage.'

"Of course, your mother heard that and went berserk. Yet she had a plan. She stayed home for a week, and then she called me and we agreed to meet the following day. She left the house, we met, and we went to the marriage registrar. We got married without telling anyone. She said that was the only way, and I guess she was right. Look, at the time she was definitely right. She then left me and went back home. There, she placed our marriage certificate on the dining table before your grandmother and told her she now had two options. One was to accept the marriage: we would have a small wedding and avoid a scandal. Or I would go and claim her by the power of law. I was, after all, her husband. Once the fights, abuse, and breakdowns had subsided, your grandmother agreed to the first option. We had a wedding and were officially married. So there you go."

I was mesmerized by that story. I couldn't believe how strong-willed and capable my mother was, or how much my father was in love with her. It was like she was a different person. The story of their marriage was inspiring for someone like me. I would often sit in my father's study, on the floor by his feet, and read their letters. He kept them in a big bundle inside a large brown envelope in his third drawer.

The three drawers in my father's desk were my magic world. In the first, he kept important documents—his ID, passport, sometimes a bit of money. The second drawer held all his prescription glasses since he was a child, a beautiful brown pipe, an old vitamin C tube where he kept copper and silver coins from different countries, binoculars that he once allowed me to use to watch a ballet at the opera, many unused packs of medicine, newspaper cuttings (probably cut out years ago, then forgotten along with their contexts), photos of me at different stages of my life, photos of us at my childhood birthdays and on the beach in Montazah and Marsa Matruh, countless photos of the woman he loved before my mother, and photos of them together in different countries—she was tall and slim and always wearing very big sunglasses. There were pictures of my father with friends all over the world—Berlin, Baghdad, London, New York, Malaysia, and other places I didn't recognize.

That second drawer was filled with details and memories that belonged to my father alone. Many things were indecipherable to me, and he always eluded my questions with an enigmatic smile. But the third drawer was my favorite. It was full of papers. Nothing but papers. A mass of handwritten papers—the large brown envelope with the letters to my mother, many unfinished stories, manuscripts of short stories that were later published, manuscripts from other writers. I liked to open that drawer while my father was asleep and read everything I could read. The third drawer was inexhaustible: I would find something new every day, new papers and new stories. All the stories were beautiful, even if most were unfinished.

10

My father taught me never to stay on the margins. I must stand firmly inside the picture and not let anyone push me to the sidelines; otherwise I might lose the desire to live and become useless. As I marched with the crowds in the direction of the Ministry of Interior, that thought filled my head. Things were heating up. Some of the young people were starting to lose their tempers in the face of the provocative, cocky smiles of the Central Security officers. I reached for my father and pulled him by the hand to make sure we walked in the middle of the march. Because of his illness and his weak heart, he wouldn't have been able to run if things turned violent, so I slowed down to give us some room for escape. We entered the street leading to the ministry. The march was huge. The chants echoed in my head, powerful and defiant. So many people and so much zeal—but all I heard were echoes, and all I saw was my father's face, his eyes bright with anticipation and awe.

The protestors started to throw stones at the security forces, or maybe it was the other way around—I wasn't sure who started it; it seemed to happen at an agreed moment. I quickly pulled my father toward a nearby building, worried I wouldn't be able to protect him. I whispered in his ear, "Let's try to leave by the back streets and pretend we were just passing through." He didn't answer and kept his eyes on the battle with growing concern. "This violence is foolish. The bastards will kill those kids."

"Bastards"—the term that always and forever, whenever it was uttered by my father, referred to the security forces, all and any security forces, in a sweeping generalization that allowed for no exceptions.

"Don't worry," I said. "Things have to calm down soon. Let's just leave."

We began to move. As I tried to determine the trajectories of stones over our heads, a small one hit my shoulder. My father panicked. "What was that? Are you hurt?"

"Not at all, Baba. It was just a pebble."

We walked until we were farther away from the action and quickened our pace as we approached Tahrir Square. By the time we got there, my father's breathing had quickened and his chest was wheezing—not at all reassuring. "Baba, you're going home now," I told him. "This is too much for you, and we have no idea what's going to happen."

"But I don't want to leave. Listen, when I get tired I'll tell you to put me in a taxi."

"Oh, so you're just going to abandon me here? I thought you would at least tell me I should go home too."

He went quiet for a few seconds, and then said, "Look, even if I tell you to leave, you never would. And I wouldn't have the heart to tell you to leave in the first place. You must stay. Stay close to where it's happening. Stay with the people. Let's see what the bastards are going to do next."

We walked around the square and kept running into friends and colleagues. My father also met friends and began to feel better; his breathing was calmer as he got into lively discussions. I stayed close to him and kept an eye on the time. The square was filling up. A skinny young man climbed a lamppost near the middle and installed a pair of big speakers. He started to say something into a microphone—his voice was distorted and barely decipherable, and I strained my ears to hear. "This is the Radio of the Revolution. Statement number one."

I didn't hear the rest because I burst out laughing. It was a revolution now, the boy had decided. Did a few thousand people in the streets of Cairo, and in some of the provinces, make a revolution? I couldn't stop laughing.

Then I heard my father's voice: "Enough now—it could be a revolution with half this number. Clearly you don't understand a thing, you pessimist. Who knows what could happen?"

"So how about you go home," I told him, "and come back if it turns out to be a revolution? I promise I would come get you myself. I'll pay for your taxi to the revolution's front door."

He was annoyed by my sarcasm, but was persuaded in the end to go home. I put him in a taxi at the edge of the square.

"Don't leave unless it gets too violent. Don't give up too soon."

"You really want to get rid of me, don't you?"

"Don't be scared of getting caught," he said in a serious tone. "I would get you out."

"Yeah, sure, because you have so many police officer friends."

"No, but I'll find people who are friends with the bastards."

I finally said good-bye to him and went back to wait for the inevitable moment of dispersion.

11

THE VEGETABLES AT THE GREENGROCER'S looked fresh. Eggplant it was, then. I selected a few of the large black ones, feeling them with both hands to make sure they were neither too soft nor too hard. They had to appeal to my sense of touch, as did the few tomatoes and green peppers I picked next. I also got baladi onions. It baffled me that some people preferred the milder shallots. There was fresh garlic, so though I was only going to need a few cloves, I picked two bulbs. With garlic in particular, I always liked to buy more than I needed. I paid and carried my plastic bags to the nearby corner store. I didn't like big supermarkets and preferred instead to go to this small store, five minutes' walk from my place. I got a large can of tomatoes, a bottle of vegetable oil for frying, another of corn oil, a large packet of salt—I was out of salt—and a medium-sized bottle of vinegar. Then I went to the butcher shop right next door. I asked for three-quarters of a kilo of ground beef and watched as the butcher pressed and minced it. The bags were getting heavier in my hands and leaving marks on my fingers. I added the bag of ground beef to my load and set off on foot. At the spice store I asked for an assortment: nutmeg, ground mint, black pepper, ground coriander, some mastic. The bags were heavy. I considered taking a taxi home, but decided to walk. There was no bakery nearby, so I thought I'd later ask the building's caretaker to get me a few loaves of baladi bread. Back home, I dropped the bags on the floor and threw myself onto the sofa. The pain I was feeling was real—it didn't go away when I rubbed my hands. The bags were on the floor before me. I closed my eyes for a moment, and when I woke up three hours later, I had no idea where I was.

You are the hope, the world, the dreams
When you're pleased I smile to the hidden days

Warda's voice would help me cook. The bags had been waiting on the floor for hours. I stood in the corner of the kitchen and unpacked them. Then I started peeling the onions. I didn't like food processors and preferred to chop the onions by hand to get the size and shape right: small cubes that were still thick enough to add substance to the recipe. To that end I would endure the tears and burning in my eyes. I placed the onion in a small saucepan with a bit of butter. Warda's voice continued to flow out of my laptop.

I love you as much as what has passed
I love you as much as what's yet to come

She could be so optimistic, Warda. Though she somehow managed to reach the heights of optimism and the depths of depression in the span of the same playlist. The onion turned golden. I added the ground beef and covered the saucepan. Now I needed to peel the eggplants. They were just right, not too soft and not too hard. I wondered if I should peel all of them, but no, six would be enough for a medium dish. Once they were peeled and sliced, I placed them in a big bowl of water and added a couple of drops of vinegar. I cut the remaining onions, the green peppers, and the tomatoes into rings, then heated some oil to fry everything.

There was a lot to think about. My relationship with Ali hadn't changed. His innocence, his passion, the fresh look in his eyes—I was still in awe of all these things. I did not tire of looking into his eyes.

I told my father about Ali and he listened with interest. "Do you love him, then?" he asked.

"I don't know. Maybe. He is just significant. You know when you feel like someone is holding on to the leg of your pants—you don't want to give him your pants but you don't want to kick him away either. You just want him to stay near you."

My father laughed at my unromantic analogy. I really wasn't sure how I had become so attached to Ali in such a short time. Maybe it was just a period of general susceptibility. There was a lot of passion in the air—demonstrations and intense emotions everywhere you looked—and we must have simply been susceptible to falling in love. Nothing was stable, and love was the opposite of stability. Ali himself was the opposite of stability.

I fried the green pepper rings. The meat was done. I ground the garlic cloves the traditional way: wrapping them in a plastic bag and crushing them using the bottom of a glass. It was a primitive method but it produced the exact consistency that I wanted. I let the garlic sizzle in a little bit of ghee, then added some vinegar for the taqliya, releasing an aroma that characterizes every Egyptian kitchen. I added the tomatoes and let the sauce simmer.

Ali almost never called. He mainly sent me text messages to say that he was or wasn't coming to see me. I barely knew what he sounded like on the phone. I would just see his name on my cell phone and find a short message, usually with the time of our next meeting, rarely accompanied by chatter of any kind. When I was done frying the vegetables, I layered the eggplant, pepper, onion, and tomato in a baking dish, mixed the garlic into the meat, added that too, then put the dish in the oven.

Count the stars
Count the people
Leave me but always come back

Warda was still singing. The aroma of moussaka filled the apartment. No one had called. No one was coming to eat with me. I wasn't really hungry. I lit a match and smoked my seventh cigarette, then turned off the oven and went to bed.

12

I COULD BARELY MOVE AROUND my apartment, which might have been the smallest studio in the world: four walls, a small corner for the kitchen, a small built-in cupboard. It took exactly seven steps to get from one end to the other. I paced within the walls of the apartment, in my shoes, patiently counting my steps, until I got bored and made the difficult decision to go out. In the elevator I avoided looking at my neighbor, who always regarded me with curiosity. I knew he was dying to know who I was and what I did for a living, but I wasn't going to let myself be pulled into small talk merely to fill the fifty seconds it took to go down eight floors. I didn't have space in my life for a transient stranger who in a few weeks or months would no longer be part of it.

I walked to the end of the quiet street until I got to the main road, noisy and full of cars and buses. Suddenly filled with panic, I turned back to the quiet street and kept walking. There were so many embassies, but I could never make out the colors of the flags, as they were all usually folded on themselves, even when it was windy. I looked up at the nice old buildings, mostly covered in soot but still beautiful, ruined only by their ugly neighbors that had been built during the Sadat era in the 1970s—ugly times those were.

Finally I stepped into the Italian café in a street parallel to mine. It was a small, modest place—I didn't know who owned it, but the fact that it had wooden columns was enough for me to frequent it. As usual, I was on my second cup of coffee before I started to look around me. There were no familiar faces, thank God. I didn't want to see anyone I knew and have to force a smile or make the effort to fill the void that came after the first greeting. I put my headphones on and plugged them into the laptop. I wondered if I should listen to ABBA or Baligh Hamdi, Georgette Sadegh or Hoda Haddad, but Fairuz was the choice I had stuck to every morning for at least ten years. She sang "Morn and Eve" while I drank my coffee until my nose reached the bottom of the cup.

I was terrified of the world that lay beyond me. That desire to be isolated from the world, from the details of streets and living beings, was constant. The imaginary lives I held within me were enough for me and the populations of a few more worlds. I wasn't exactly indifferent to life, just to this particular life. Stories of other worlds appealed to me: magical galaxies with different planets and different creatures. I regularly read NASA reports to feed my dreams of travel to other worlds. One day I was going to have my own mini-planet. I would be a wrinkled old woman by then, possibly senile and suffering from dementia, with hardly enough brain cells left to process the new mini-planet I would reside on. Nonetheless, I would build a room on it and paint all the walls dark purple and put up photos of all the people and all the places I love and organize my mementos in small boxes on shelves, like I did everywhere I went.

I stared at the wall before me. Fairuz sang about a tall, fenced-in pigeon tower. The sky outside the café's window had darkened. It was time to go back to my tiny home.

13

I SIT ON THE EDGE of my sofa for days or weeks, maybe months, detached from the details of everyday life, just contemplating and anticipating, thinking mostly depressing thoughts. Maybe I have lost that yearning for the unknown that I used to have. Fearless, they used to call me. I was going to do whatever I wanted: visit unknown lands, explore orange rivers, arid fields, and soft mountains. I was going to run with all my might toward the unknown. Travel was going to be my destination, and passion for the unknown my prayer.

I do not want to settle. Settling would be my death. I do not want to know what might happen, where I might go, who I might wander down dreamy roads with, sharing an innocent moment of stolen happiness.

Maybe I'd visit neatly paved roads like those we see in French children's movies, or find myself in a town where they speak only Swahili. I could watch stories unfold around me and not understand a word. Maybe tomorrow I would be drinking coffee in a sub-Saharan town, with a view of the Victoria Falls, wild animals roaming the unfamiliar spaces around me. Or I might find myself living an impossible romance with an unattainable lover. I'm always drawn toward the impossible, particularly in desperate love stories, like my story with Ali. Dramatic stories, full of pleasure but with no stability. I don't ever want to settle—not in love or in place. I don't want to settle politically or domestically. Sit-ins, strikes, and protests make me happy. Unfinished stories inspire me. Regular, happy family gatherings make me nervous. Hurricanes and rainstorms bring me back to life.

But I'm edging toward thirty and I still haven't found any soft mountains or orange rivers. I still haven't dyed my hair blue like Kate Winslet in that movie. I haven't jumped out of a plane, held only by a rope; maybe I would discover the secrets of the universe or the rope would break, leaving me to a gentle fall. I haven't met kings or slaves; I haven't lain on my back on smooth ice that would either break and swallow me, or hold me and let me watch a sky full of stars. I haven't seen the world from the top of a mountain or from the depths of the ocean. Nor sipped the local coffee of every country in the world. Nor held hands with a man in every city and been told there was no one like me, and then cried at the moment of parting.

I still haven't lived a single story to match my fantasies or the books I've read.

I lay on that sofa for weeks—or was it months?—and got lost in a maze of repetitive thoughts. I was bored—bored and settled—settled on the sofa, and settled in my lack of passion and longing. I was settled with Ali and because of him. We spoke at certain times, and met at certain times. When the times came, I rose with difficulty out of my long slumber to change my clothes. He might or might not have noticed my outfits, but I changed anyway, with calm, mechanical movements. For the first time in my nearly thirty years I knew exactly what was going to happen next: the passion of the first moments, the sacred embrace at the door, then food and maybe some boring TV, very few words, a little arguing over details that reflect our dull lives, then sleep.

What did Ali see in me, I still wonder. Was I a reflection of what he wanted but lacked the energy to do? Was I just some girl with whom he woke up one day, and because he found his hand holding her wrist he decided to hold on to that moment until he got bored? Did he see me as successful and accomplished? Did I represent a vague idea to him? Did I arouse his curiosity? Or just his desire? I didn't know why he stayed. And I had no idea when he would decide to leave. That might have been the only unknown in the simple and settled life we led.

My dreams of colorful mountains and vigorous waterfalls were gone. I got used to seeing my awaited cosmos in Ali's eyes. I didn't collect clippings and photos of mysterious places to stick on the walls any more, in anticipation of the day when I would carry my backpack and go. Had I really stopped dreaming? Maybe I had just lost my private dream worlds, and the stories and imagined details about people I was yet to meet. I still dreamed, but only in whirlpools of repetitive and predictable events. I didn't want anything more than the worlds and people I saw in Ali's eyes. That was my compensation for the imagination I had lost. His eyes were imagination itself. All his disappointments, defeats, and perpetual confusion disappeared in those moments of serenity when his eyes sparkled and became windows on the world.

I wanted to take him with me to the soft, colorful mountains. I wanted us to dip our hands together into the orange river. I wanted to lie on the roof with him and watch the stars, both fixed and falling, in a sky clear of pollution and smoke. Neither of us belonged here—in these closed circles, fixed appointments, and routines emptied of all spontaneity and wildness. We didn't belong on this sofa that was swallowing our bodies. I saw us all the time, with what little imagination I had left, entering foreign realms and meeting new people. I saw us dancing to unfamiliar songs in foreign languages. I saw us in cities at the edge of the world, waiting for rain, and our childlike glee when the raindrops wet our faces and roused us out of the dryness of the lives we led. So I waited for him, and the fear of boredom filled me. I was scared that boredom would bring us to our end and leave us to regret all the things we did not do. I waited for the real Ali, waited for the passion and curiosity in his eyes to replace the look of fear and sometimes suspicion that had taken over.

He was who he was: reckless and wretched, with the imagination of a child. I was who I was: willing to sell my soul to a mercenary wizard on a street corner for the sake of a new experience. We were just ourselves, and we owned nothing. From curiosity we came and to curiosity we would return. We had no plans, and lived only for those moments of absolute joy, of abandoned laughter, a meditative vision, or one second of innocent awe. Maybe we were miserable because of the historical moment. Or maybe because he was at a crossroads in his life. It was as if we lived in a context that was devoid of our truths. I couldn't know how long that limited course would run before we were drained of our will to live. The only truth I knew—and knew that he knew—was this: we would end a thousand times, in anguish or in boredom, in silence or in tumult, but after every ending, we would return to begin again.

14

It was going to be a decisive day, and I was anxious. I put on a thick hoodie, and in my bag I carried a water bottle and, reluctantly, a small onion. I couldn't call anyone. The "bastards" had cut off all communication. I took a taxi from Zamalek to Heliopolis, where I found my father having breakfast on the balcony. It was still an innocent morning.

"Did you read the paper today?" he asked me.

"No," I answered. "Is there anything other than the usual garbage?"

He read a few *al-Ahram* headlines out to me: "Muslim Brotherhood elements call for demonstrations and security forces succeed in foiling the intrigues of the banned group. Cautious calm returns to city streets. Security forces on standby in case of renewed protests. Renewed protests in Suez demand better wages. One hundred million pounds in losses to the municipality due to vandalism, fire, and looting. Freedom of expression is guaranteed. Chaos will not be tolerated."

I interrupted him. "Baba, tell you what—I've heard enough. Go get dressed, or are you not coming with me?"

"OK, OK. I'm getting up."

It didn't take my father long to get ready. We stopped a taxi outside the house and headed to Tahrir Square. My father stared out of the car window, and I wished I could read his mind. What did he think of what was happening? He must have been frightened. His health would not allow him to run if he needed to. But I was not going to let go of his hand; that I was sure of. In all honesty, though, I was terrified. We were facing the Unknown, with a capital U. We had no idea what might happen. There was hardly anyone on the roads except the Central Security forces. The taxi dropped us in Abd al-Moneim Riyad Square. Who were all those burly men? The first scene, not far from us: two of them falling on a skinny young man. I will never forget the sight of that kid under their boots. After beating him senseless, they dragged him to the Central Security van parked under the bridge.

I turned to my father. "That's it. You're going home."

"Oh, you've decided for me?" He was driving me mad with his calmness.

"Please, for my sake. It's only the start of the day, and you can see how it's going. Tell you what—I'll take you back to my place. So you'll be close by, and then you can spend the night with me."

My father could tell that I was on the verge of hysterics, or maybe he really agreed that his health would not be up to this kind of day. We walked to the bridge and waited for a few minutes for a taxi. I accompanied him to my apartment and made sure he was settled in front of the TV. "Baba, you know where everything is. You can make tea if you want. There's a chicken in the fridge. Reheat it in the oven when you're hungry. You need to eat so you can take your medication. I'll be back tonight. Don't worry, OK?"

His face was suddenly overtaken with concern. He gripped my arm. "Take care of yourself. I mean it! I couldn't handle anything happening to you. I only agreed to come back here for your sake. But take care of yourself and don't be reckless. Run if there's trouble. Running is sometimes the bravest thing to do, you understand?"

I laughed and hugged him. "Don't worry about me. I'm a coward anyway."

"No, you're not a coward. You can be reckless and unpredictable. But for my sake, you'll take care of yourself today."

I smiled as I closed the door behind me and headed back to the Unknown.

When I got back that night, I was pretty much a wreck, so tired my feet could barely carry me. I was covered in dust, and sticky because of all the soda we'd been pouring on our faces to neutralize the pain of tear gas. My long straight hair somehow managed to look like a toilet brush; it was completely disheveled. My eyes, like millions of eyes that day, were red and swollen because of the tear gas. I looked like I had stepped out of the grave.

My father opened the door. "Where have you been, damn you! I was worried sick!" He pulled me into an anxious hug. "Are you OK? Do you have any injuries? Did something happen to you? Tell me!"

"Baba, just give me a minute to breathe. I can hardly stand. I'll tell you everything."

I threw myself onto the small sofa and began to tell my father about the day.

"After I left you I decided not to take a taxi. I walked to the Opera House and into a massive demonstration. I marched with them. The chants were amazing—loud and powerful and full of defiance. Anyway, we got to Qasr al-Nil Bridge. There was constant tear gas, coming from all directions. It nearly blinded me. At first I rubbed my eyes, which made them burn more. The more they burned, though, the angrier I became and the more determined I was to go on. So, we were at the bridge. Then all hell broke loose. If only I knew where they were shooting from. It seemed like the gas canisters were dropping from everywhere. Everywhere. Five or six at a time, the bastards. I couldn't control where I was going, but was just being carried along with the crowd. Everyone seemed to be pushing in the opposite direction of the bridge. I had no idea what was going on. Were we trying to cross the bridge to get to the square? Were we trying to turn back because there was no way to cross? I couldn't move. So I breathed in the tear gas and chanted."

I went on, watching the changing emotions on my father's face: "Some people were starting to lose it. A boy who looked about eighteen was trying to break one of the lampposts on the bridge. Then someone else stopped him and said that was public property, and the boy broke down crying. By that point, the Central Security cars had blocked both ends of the bridge. I thought that was it. It was obviously a trap. I can't swim, but thought about jumping into the Nile anyway. All I could think of then was that I could not possibly go on. I was never going to make it to either end of the bridge, and it was blocked anyway, so what was the point? I could hardly see anything. Some kids had started to set fire to the Central Security vans. I won't lie. I was really scared. I thought the vans would explode once they'd caught fire, and if they exploded, the whole bridge would go up in flames.

"Anyway, the vans didn't explode. But the smoke mixed with the tear gas was so strong. What tipped me over the edge, though, was when some of the boys did not want to let the soldiers out of the vans, and I started screaming, 'Let them out! Please let them out! We can't let them die in there!' It was very dramatic, but the thought had filled me with panic. Those of us who wanted to save the soldiers won in the end, and they let them out. You know, Baba, they were like scared rabbits. They came out with their hands on the backs of their heads like prisoners of war. An escape route was created behind the vans, so that the soldiers could immediately leave the bridge. Otherwise people would have eaten them alive. They'd been shooting at us all day long. All day long we'd been withstanding beatings and tear gas and birdshot, which can cause a lot of damage. Not to mention the live bullets we could hear throughout the day. It was one long horror movie."

My father asked, "Were you alone all that time?"

"Oh no, I met everyone I know on that bridge. Almost everyone I know was there. But I would see people for a couple of minutes, then lose them. They would run or be pulled away. You don't get it. It was a massive battle—massive!"

He listened, awed and apprehensive, then said, "I saw things on TV but couldn't understand what was happening. I had to be out there. I shouldn't have stayed home like a baby. Fuck this weak health and this weak heart of mine!"

I tried to distract him. "Have you eaten?"

"Yes. What else could I do? I had to take the damn medicine. Go on."

So I went on: "Once all the vans were burned, things calmed down a little, or that's what I thought. I left the bridge and met some friends and walked with them toward the square. The sun was setting. Something odd was going on. The security forces were almost nowhere to be seen. The sky was filled with smoke. People were still chanting, and I'll tell you something—at one point I was leading the chant. People chanted after me, even though my voice was high-pitched and silly.

"I didn't get to the square in the end. Smoke was coming out of the big building on the corniche, Mubarak's party headquarters. It was on fire. People were running out of it carrying stuff. I was on the other side of the road. I could hardly stand, but couldn't walk either. People were carrying chairs, computers, documents, and desk lamps out of the building. Just random stuff.

"And all around me on the street, people made predictions: a curfew, a presidential speech, and all sorts of other things. But I panicked when they said the army was deployed. I mean, shit, the army! Were they going to shoot at us out of tanks now?"

"Yes, I saw the tanks and armored vehicles on TV. My heart nearly stopped."

"Keep that evil thought away," I said, waving away the bad omen. "I wanted to run, you know. I mean, Central Security vans and guards and officers—we can handle those. But the army! I had only ever seen armored vehicles at the Sixth of October Museum! Anyway, for some reason people decided to deal with the situation like it was a wedding or a mulid festival. They started running toward the tanks, climbing on top of them, hugging the army soldiers, and chanting *for* them! I didn't really get it, but my feeling was that people were so scared and tired they decided to embarrass the army into friendliness!"

The TV droned on with the news as I told my story. I was quiet for a few moments, then realized I didn't have the strength to tell any more. I had seen a lot of blood that day. I didn't share all the details with my father. I didn't tell him about the boy's blood that, while a bit fainter now, still stained my clothes. I was close to him when he fell, and it was no stray bullet that hit him. I did not want to touch him. I did not want to touch the blood. But he almost fell into my arms. He was already dead. The bullet had gotten him in the chest, in the heart, I'm not sure, but he died immediately. His blood was on my clothes. That was all I worried about. My heart was beating all over the place. A bystander had lifted me off him, shouting, "The boy's dead! The boy's dead, you dogs!" This wasn't the first dead boy, but he was the first whose blood stained me. I crawled away on my hands and knees and stood up at the edge of the crowd. I visualized throwing myself into the river, but I didn't do it. I had to get back to my father. I had to tell him what I had seen and reassure him that I was OK.

I didn't throw myself off. Maybe I should have. But I didn't.

15

I READ A LOT ABOUT the prison years in the sixties. Most of that generation of intellectuals spent about five years in detention, in what my father called the 1959 roundup. Leftist intellectuals and, of course, Muslim Brothers, and others who had nothing to do with anything. My father was among the naive ones who managed to get arrested again after they were released in 1964, in what he called "the more famous political roundup." He was reluctant to speak about it, yet when he did, it was always with the same smile. Prison nostalgia: a longing I never understood. I would draw the details out of him, trying to imagine what the cell looked like, how he slept, what he wore—trying to erase from my mind all clichés about prison. Did he wear a blue uniform like we saw in movies? He never told me. His stories were always about his fellow prisoners. I was a child and knew none of the names he mentioned.

But one story I've always remembered is that of Fouad Haddad, who wrote poetry. He slept in the top bunk and would hang upside down so my father would see his head from the bottom bunk. Hanging there, he stood his poetry on its head too: He always wrote the last lines of a new poem first. That story amused me. My father, on the other hand, was sad when he wrote. He rested his forehead on one hand while he wrote with the other.

When I sat on his lap, he would put his arm around me and keep on writing. Sometimes he would give me a kiss; sometimes I would scribble on the paper he was using in order to get his attention. He would laugh and say, "Scribble all you like. Rip up all the papers you want. That's what I had you for. You rip away and I start again." I would go quiet and watch him write, then climb down and go to my room.

I was deeply saddened when Abd al-Wahhab died. I thought I would mourn him alone. No one else in our home cared much for him. In all honesty, I didn't like him on a personal level; I just liked the stories he shared and responded to. But then I was surprised when I found my father crying bitterly. He never read Abd al-Wahhab's column, so why was he crying? I asked. He looked at me with annoyance: "It's Abd al-Wahhab the musician who died, Nadia! Not Abd al-Wahhab Mutawei who writes the agony column!"

"Oh," I replied, "the 'Nagwa' guy?"

"Nagwa" was the title of a poem that my father had listened to Abd al-Wahhab sing on a daily basis for years. The word means an intimate conversation, but it can also be a woman's name, so I—not understanding a word of the poem back then—assumed it was about a woman.

If the sad night holds me, I am moved by Nagwa

It must have evoked a certain memory for my father. It's a depressing poem that Abd al-Wahhab makes even more depressing in song. He must have been really moved by Nagwa. So it was *that* Abd al-Wahhab who died when I was nine years old, and not the one who entertained me with other people's problems in the newspaper. Later, I would of course regret that short-lived relief, when I really discovered Abd al-Wahhab and became even more obsessed with his songs than my father was.

16

MY TEENAGE YEARS WERE DIFFICULT. There was no one I was close to. I stood on my own two feet and pushed everyone away. Even my father. Most probably I was beginning to understand the problems of our home around that time; the painful silence between my parents, for instance. The love story that my father often retold with a bitter smile was present in my memory. My mother told the story too, blaming herself at every other sentence.

"I married your father against my mother's wishes and paid the price. She was right. As you see, he does nothing but sit at his desk all day. He doesn't even utter my name any more. I should have married a teacher or a lawyer. They would have at least talked to me."

She always complained about my father's silence, that he was constantly preoccupied by his papers and books, that he hardly spoke to her and didn't involve himself in trivial household matters. Years and years later I understood—despite my difficult relationship with my mom, who used to say that I was "spoiled like my father"—that sometimes a woman needs a man who goes grocery shopping with her and argues with the vegetable seller over a few pennies for a kilo of potatoes. He was a cultured man with a superior intellect, as she used to say, but he never talked to her.

My father didn't talk to me either during my teenage years. He was sometimes affectionate with me, reluctantly. I knew he was feeling affectionate when he called me "Nannous." I would smile and say I was too old. Then he would put on a deep frown and say, "What do you mean too old? You'll stay a little girl forever, even when you're a hundred years old. Too old! You'll always be my Nannous." So I would surrender and go sit in my father's arms as he went on reading, with a smile on his face. Other than that, I lived inside my own personal bubble. I would put on the headphones of my Walkman, a pretty red one that my father's friend had gotten for me from the US. I would turn the volume up to its maximum and listen to rock music. The loud rhythms and guitar shocked my mother and soothed me.

I listened to Guns 'N' Roses and Metallica and Bon Jovi, but also to ABBA, which my father liked. I knew the words to "Chiquitita" and would sing them when he could hear me so he would know I was no longer a child. I was listening to the same songs that a grown man like him liked. I listened to Nagat and Sayed Darwish and Mohamed Fawzy, and to pop music, and I knew all of Michael Jackson's songs by heart. I put on black nail polish and pretended to look like an American rock chick, but was let down by my long straight hair.

A true rock chick's hair was curly and messy. I listened to everything. I knew Munir's songs by heart and didn't see any contradiction between that and standing before the rock star posters in my room, holding the broom as a guitar and head banging, or being moved by the sensitive Abd al-Halim, by the story of his illness and by his tender, almost pity-arousing, voice. I hardly ever took my headphones off, despite my mother's yelling and my father's reproachful looks, both urging me to turn the volume down a little.

No one understood me. Every teenager has the right to feel that way. I was completely alone. I didn't like my schoolmates and daydreamed about the school collapsing on their heads, killing everyone but me and Radwa.

Radwa was my only friend. She understood me and approved of the Slash poster that had pride of place on my wardrobe door. Radwa knew me, and we did everything together—we were silent together, skipped school together, read trashy novels together, and hated everyone together. I liked going to Radwa's house, and Mom let me go as often as I liked, because Radwa was clever and got good grades and "if only you could be like her." I went over to Radwa's on weekends to listen to rock music—which she didn't really like but listened to for my sake—and eat fries that her father made for us, and browse her little home library. I would usually bring a few books from my little library—or rather my father's, which he let me share—and we'd swap. She also had a little gerbil that she bought at a pet shop in Heliopolis. She would say mysteriously that it was her guinea pig, then add with affected innocence, "But I wouldn't do any experimentation on him. I wouldn't want him to die." Her mother hated the gerbil and hoped he would escape, but was too disgusted by the animal to open the cage it lived in.

The main difference between Radwa and me was her passion for science. She did really do some silly experiments at home. She would steal things from the school's laboratory, buy strange liquids, put it all in test tubes, and stare admiringly at the colors and vapors. I thought she was insane, until she ended up as a successful surgeon at a big hospital on the other side of the world. She was strange: she not only liked physics and chemistry, but also got excited about surgery.

So I put on rock music tapes in the little cassette player next to the balcony in her room and painted my nails black, while she poured liquids into test tubes. Then we both read stories and hated the world together.

My mother died when I was fourteen years old. She died suddenly. The doctor from the public hospital next to our house wrote "heart attack" on the death certificate, but that's probably what all doctors write when they have no real explanation. I didn't cry, which was normal for me. I never cried, not as a child nor as a teenager. My father didn't let me attend the washing of the body. He thought it was too much for a girl my age, and I didn't insist. More than anything I was curious about my father's reaction to my mother's death. He surprised me, as usual, by crying silently at her burial. I didn't understand why he cried. I was sure he had stopped loving her ages ago. His tears confused me. I had seen him cry in silence once before, while poring over his papers. But seeing him cry on the day of the burial was more confusing and left me nervous and distressed.

After my mother's death, the shape of our lives changed. I had new responsibilities. Cooking for myself and my father was relatively easy, but my father also decided I was now the lady of the house—he insisted on sharing all the particulars of the household expenses with me. He wrote down the different items of expenditure in small handwriting in a little notebook:

Newspapers
Rent
Butcher
Garbage collection
Electricity
Nadia's pocket money
Medicine
School fees
Schoolbooks
School uniform

My father's salary wasn't great, but it was enough. He was proud of the fact that we didn't need help from anyone and didn't want for anything and that we got to that without him ever accepting a bribe or stealing or doing anything we would (both) regret later. Life wasn't unhappy. My father talked all the time. I listened to him in silence, as he told me unending stories about his childhood, his father, his sisters, and his prison years in the sixties. He also told me about his travels, the long travels and the short travels. He didn't often talk about my mother, but sometimes he did. He talked about his previous lovers, describing them in detail, and sometimes opening his second drawer to get out photos to supplement his stories. I was mostly silent, but sometimes I asked questions, and I always enjoyed the stories. I linked arms with him as we sat on our blue sofa and he talked and talked until I fell asleep.

I didn't abandon my father. But it was necessary to leave. Since I was a kid I'd been against the idea that a girl goes straight from her father's house to her husband's house. I did not abandon my father in his illness and old age. I just wanted to break away from that norm. He'd known me since I was in my mother's womb: he knew my restlessness that had kept her awake at night. He knew I couldn't sit still in a place that I hadn't chosen of my own volition. I sat him down and informed him of my decision. I was a grown-up now. I worked in a big company and had a good salary that would allow me to pay rent on a small apartment. He was pensive for a few moments, then: "You want to leave me, Nadia?"

I was moved. "No, I don't want to leave you at all. Moving out doesn't mean leaving you. I'll come visit every day, and you will come and stay over, two or three times a week. I won't leave you. And please don't pressure me."

"I'm not pressuring you. I know I can't. When I was little, I was always first out the door for school. I would stop in front of the train station and look at the trains, and think to myself that as soon as I had money I'd run away and go to Cairo. I felt suffocated by the village where we lived, not because it was a bad place but because I hadn't chosen to live in it. I know you don't hate our home, but you need to do your own thing."

I got up and hugged him. "So do I have your blessing?"

"Because not having it would have stopped you?"

"Yes. If you said to me honestly and directly that you didn't want me to go, I'd stay."

That annoyed him a bit. "Because you know I'd never do that!"

"All's good then," I said. "How much will you contribute?"

He gave me a tight smile. "You're in charge of the household money, Nadia. See how much you need and work it out. When are you planning to move out? Have you found a place yet?"

"I haven't started looking. I wanted to talk to you first. So I'm thinking that maybe in, like, three months I will have sorted something out."

I could see a trace of sadness in his face. I didn't want to be the cause of that sadness, but I had made up my mind. I would pack up my stuff and have a new place, a new start, and I'd create on my own all that came with it.

My father couldn't live alone for long, so he moved in with my aunts in Heliopolis. They were widows who lived together and didn't mind him joining them. He didn't know how to live alone. I continued to manage his monthly expenses even after I moved out. I found my small studio and bought my beloved sofa, which became my cocoon. I would lie within it like a tortoise in her shell. I only worked when I ran out of money and had to pay the rent. I didn't have many needs. I bought things I didn't need when my wallet was full, and when it was empty I stayed at home, in the cocoon of my sofa. I watched old movies on TV, and smiled childishly when Zaynat Sedky cornered Ismail Yassin in the kitchen of *Ibn Hamido.*

17

When I was twelve, two years before my mother's sudden death, Radwa and I decided one day that we wouldn't take the school bus and would walk back home instead. I told her that was madness; that it would be a long walk and it was very hot, and then there would be a fight with our mothers at home when they found out about what we'd done. She laughed carelessly and said, "But they fight with us anyway. Don't worry, we'll walk fast and won't be that late." Deep down I wanted to go with her so I didn't resist much, just mumbled some objections.

We walked for over two hours, holding hands and crossing streets, jumping on and off sidewalks, laughing loudly. Out of breath, with our heavy schoolbags on our backs, we stopped every once in a while for a few minutes' break, then kept on walking. It was my first time to walk independently in the street.

"You know what I want us to do?" I asked Radwa. "I want us, one day, to walk and walk, at night, and stay out all night until the sun comes out."

She laughed. "One day we will. But when we grow up, so that we're allowed out at night. But I promise you we'll do it one day—you remember that."

"And we'll walk to the other side of the big bridge and go to the midnight cinema," I said.

That was the height of my ambition—to stay up till morning in the streets of Downtown, walking with Radwa until our feet hurt, with not a care in the world, no fight at the end of the adventure and no calculations needed to avoid it.

Years later, when I went to visit her during a snowy winter where she lived and worked on the other side of the globe, we thought back to that day. We sat together on a sidewalk in a large square and watched all sorts of people walking in hurried steps around us. No one noticed that we sat on the ground. No one harassed us with any annoying pseudo-flirty remarks like we would have heard back home.

"Men here are certainly not like men in Egypt," I joked. "I mean, there's no one harassing us or accosting us or making our lives hell."

"Yep. Everyone ignores each other here."

Surprised, I asked, "Does it bother you?"

"No, of course not," she said. "But sometimes I just wish someone, anyone, would talk to me. Sometimes I go for days without talking at all."

I saw bitterness in her eyes, which hadn't been there when we were younger. She was outgoing and sardonic and had an ability to cope with anything. It must have been the loneliness.

In this strange country, Radwa and I went out and danced in bars we didn't know and where no one knew our names. We made fun of everyone. We remembered our teenage years, her little gerbil, the headphones of my red Walkman. We remembered how we hated school. We drank everything we could afford. When men chatted us up, we frowned and consulted with each other in Arabic, then smiled and danced with the strangers. When it got late and everyone left, we decided to walk home. We walked and walked until our feet hurt, only to discover that we had been circling her house for two hours. Time flew and carried us home and we slept with childish tired smiles on our faces. The next day we would go to the cinema, then walk around town, or maybe we would take the bus or the train to another town. We were going to spend our days doing what we wanted, without thinking too hard about anything, until it was time to leave again.

I used Radwa's phone to call my father. It was a bad line.

"How are you? I really miss you. Are you well?"

"I've missed you so much, Nadia. When will you be back?"

"Not long now. Only a few more days. Are you OK? How's your heart? It hasn't been acting up, has it?"

He laughed. "What do you care? Didn't you choose Radwa's company over mine?"

"Baba, stop fooling around. I need to know how you're doing."

"Yes, my love, I'm fine," he said with tenderness. "My health is perfectly fine. How's Radwa?"

"She's good. Dissecting people at the hospital all day and roaming around with me all night." I finished the phone call with my father and found Radwa smoking by the window, with a pensive look on her face.

"What is it?" I asked.

"I've really missed your father. I'd give anything to have one of my old chats with him."

"Well, I miss him too," I said with a tight smile. "Come back to Egypt, then at least we'll be together."

"Maybe. Maybe we'll all meet again one day."

She blew out the smoke of her cigarette.

That winter I spent New Year's Eve with Radwa. We took the bus from her small town, and three hours later we were in New York City. We had all our winter clothes on: scarves and hats, two heavy sweaters each, and woolen socks to keep our feet from freezing. I shivered in the cold and she told me she'd seen worse. "This is nothing. You need to toughen up." When we stepped off the bus, she started to run and jump in the street. I told her I'd slip and break my neck if I did the same. My fingers trembled when I lit my first cigarette. When I pulled a hand out of its woolen glove, I felt all the blood leave it. I smoked less than half the cigarette and put it out quickly to return my hand to its glove.

We went to a pizza place and found that it was run by an Egyptian guy. He shouted over to us: "Dessert is on the house, girls! Happy New Year!" We laughed, and she said I was a magnet for Egyptians wherever I went. We walked together down New York's busy streets. There was an air of festivity everywhere.

"So what's our plan?" I asked when we stopped for a little rest. I was rubbing my hands together in the hope of generating some heat.

"I don't know. We'll just stay out until the sun comes up."

"What sun? There's never any sun in this place."

"Oh, don't be so miserable!" she exclaimed as she got up, forcing me to move fast to keep up with her. "Come, let's go get coffee."

We drank our coffee and laughed, posed for photos with random people in the street, then decided to head to Times Square, which I only knew from the movies. "I want to watch the New Year's celebration in Times Square," I declared. "Isn't there a big ball they drop at midnight?"

"Oh, it's a stupid ball and stupid Americans cheering," was Radwa's initial response.

But I insisted: "I want to go. I haven't put all my savings into a plane ticket to come all the way here and leave without seeing the ball—or Times Square, that is."

She laughed and relented. "OK, then let's go now. It gets busy."

We stood around watching the celebrations and enjoying the loud music. I counted my money and found I only had a few dollars left. I sighed and told Radwa, "If only we weren't so poor, we would have been at some glamorous party."

She replied cheerfully, “There’s nothing more glamorous than this. We’re sitting on the sidewalk waiting for your ball. Aren’t you having fun?”

I punched her shoulder jokingly and hugged her. “Well, at least we’re together.”

My phone rang. It was a call from Egypt.

“Hello . . . What’s wrong with your voice? . . . What happened? . . . OK, OK, calm down . . . Are you crying? . . . Shit . . . When was that? . . . Just calm down.” I got cut off.

Radwa asked anxiously, “What’s wrong?”

So I told her about the bomb that had gone off in a church in Alexandria a few hours earlier. There were no details yet, but it sounded terrible. We were silent for some moments.

“Did you say many people died?”

“It seems so. ”

She sighed. “That country will never get rid of its filth.”

“Don’t say that,” I scolded. “There are people who are willfully keeping it filthy. Damn them all to hell. It has to end one day.”

We tried to forget the news and enjoy the rest of the night, but our happiness was tainted. The clock struck midnight. We hugged each other but made sure not to get too emotional.

18

My father wanted to go to the countryside. I had only been there a handful of times—usually only for weddings or funerals—and didn't know it well at all. I just knew that we had a large family there, with branches of grandparents and aunts and uncles and cousins, and their children and grandchildren. My father's family was not the richest in town, but it was big and well-connected. I knew that having roots in the province of Sharqiya meant I was a "Sharqawi." It's a place known for its generosity, a town that is said to have once invited all the passengers of a train for the Ramadan meal. I often invoked this legend, as my only connection to the countryside of my origins.

My father called me early one morning. "I'm going to the countryside tomorrow and you're coming with me."

I tried in vain to persuade him to postpone, so I could make travel arrangements, but he said, "We'll go by car."

Of course we'd go by car—I didn't drive and he had stopped driving a while back. "What car, Baba? Who will drive?"

"We'll get a driver," he insisted.

I knew how much he loved road trips and how he used to take long ones when he lived abroad. I remembered when he took me and Mom to faraway summer holiday destinations and insisted on driving there. He used to say that a whole world went by outside a car's window, and he liked to see that world so that one day he would return to it.

I booked a small car with a driver and headed the following morning to Heliopolis. My father came down with a small bag, his face full of enthusiasm. I knew this pre-travel enthusiasm quite well. But I was irritated already. I didn't know why we were going or how many days we were going for. My father got into the car and proceeded to give the driver directions. Then he glued his face to the window and started to chat without looking at me. He talked about traveling by car, about trees and fields and cows, about narrow country roads and rural towns, about the coffeehouse on a street named after the post office, where he used to hang out as a teenager and which was no longer there. A modern multistory building stood in its place now. He talked about his teenage years, about his unrequited love for his friend's sister and the notes he left at her door; about his grandfather, and about his uncle who had gone to Germany on a scholarship and come back a qualified doctor, but had also become arrogant and dull. He talked and talked, then went quiet for a few minutes as he stared out the window.

I yawned. I needed to get one hour of sleep before we got to the village. But I wasn't allowed that hour.

"Wake up, don't sleep," said my father, shaking me awake. "I want to tell you about your hometown and your people. Wake up. You sleep for hours on end in Cairo. This is no time for sleeping."

"But you've told me these stories a million times before," I said. "Is it not enough for you that you're dragging me at such short notice? Please let me have a little rest."

"No, I won't let you. Wake yourself up so you don't arrive in the village with your eyes full of sleep."

He returned to his never-ending stories: coffeehouses and schools and streets, the big house his grandfather built in Zagazig where his maternal uncle continued to live with his children until they were all married, and those who were widowed returned to the same house, and how proud his uncle was that he'd never left his father's house, how he restored and renovated it every few years. And about his uncle's wife and her big, fat butt. He laughed as he described how she would knock vases over and sweep dishes off tables when she tried to move around in a small space. So I joked about how all the women in our family seemed to share that attribute.

He talked and talked, then stopped and sighed. "Those were the days." He said his village used to be a small hamlet, and when we finally got there, he added scathingly, "All towns have changed. Alexandria is not what it used to be. Mansura and Sohag now attract tourists. Everything has changed except in Zagazig, where every millimeter stays the same."

I mumbled, "Nothing ever stays the same."

We finally got to the house—my great-grandfather's home that became my great-uncle's home and was now transformed into the extended family home again. It resembled the house in Heliopolis that my grandfather had built for his children and grandchildren, and where my widowed father and aunts were now living.

We went in and were received by a straight-backed old woman wearing a black gallabiya with a pattern of blue flowers and a headscarf that only covered a small portion of her clean, cotton-like hair. My father hugged her and kissed her shoulder. I, of course, did not remember her.

"Rawya, do you remember my daughter Nadia?" he asked her.

She hugged me and said, with seeming familiarity, "Of course I remember you. You've grown up so much, Nadia!"

I smiled as she kissed me.

As we sat in the big reception hall, my father whispered to me that Rawya was his uncle's eldest daughter. It was suffocatingly hot and there were many insects sticking to my skin. But in order to avoid trouble with my father, I tried not to look grumpy. There were several children playing in the courtyard. They wore dirty clothes, and looked like they would have been cleaner and more presentable at an earlier stage of the morning.

I asked the old woman if I could use the bathroom to wash off the dust and sweat from the road. She leaned on my arm and led me to the bathroom, then stood at the door and handed me a clean towel. The bathroom had the refreshing smell of old-fashioned soap. The tiles on the floor were old but spotless. "Have you finished college, Nadia?" the old lady asked me. I wasn't sure how to address her—the Cairene word 'tante' would fall flat in this environment, and—as she was related to my father on his mother's side—I didn't know which would be more suitable, the word for maternal or paternal aunt. I opted for the latter, and said with a nervous smile, "Yes, Ammeto, I've finished."

"And have you gotten married?"

"Not yet." I didn't dare tell her that I lived on my own, like loose girls did.

I expected, as the soap forced me to close my eyes, to hear a lecture about the dangers of spinsterhood and the necessity of marriage for girls, but instead she said wisely, "Good. Don't rush it. Where does marriage get you in the end? My girls got married early and their grandchildren are playing outside. But it was all hardship. Enjoy your life, my girl. There's duck and roasted potatoes for lunch, so good you and your father will lick your plates clean."

When I opened my eyes she was gone.

I returned to find my father sitting with a group of ordinary-looking men and women. The women were moderately beautiful, and all were in their sixties or a bit older. Rawya was the oldest one in the house. She might have been the last one remaining from her generation. I imagined that she was over ninety. Her health seemed good and her eyes were lively.

She reminded me of my eldest aunt—her skin was wrinkled and her arms as thin as a skeleton's but her eyes were full of a natural intelligence.

I greeted everyone in the group affectionately. The women hugged me and the men smiled and shook my hand. I sat next to my father, who was asking them about their news and that of other relatives. Every now and then someone would say, "But he died years ago." And my father would reply, "That's God's will." The names of so many dead made my heart sink.

The old woman called me to help her in the kitchen. All the women had gone in to help. But first she showed me around the house. There were so many rooms, big and airy. She opened one and said, "This is my husband's room, God rest his soul. Everything here is as it was." It was a big room, all wood, with a giant bed and wardrobe, a clean rug, the smell of incense, prayer beads on the bedside table—it felt like no one ever entered it. "When he died, God rest his soul, his brother wanted us to sell the house and give him his share of the inheritance. The house would have sold for a lot of money. But I stood up to him. I told him: 'This is my grandfather's house and there's nothing for you here except hospitality when you visit. But your share? Your share in this house is the toilet, nothing more. You want to sell the toilet? Let me see you do that!' He thought I was insolent, but I won. This room is cleaned every day. As you can see, it sparkles."

I nodded in agreement.

She took me toward a wooden staircase in the middle of another hall inside the house and opened a wooden door that was invisible until you opened it. "This is the magic room. We called it that because your great-grandfather built it inside the staircase. When we were little, anyone who entered this room got a beating. It was his private room, and he could indulge in his vice of choice without being seen." She laughed. "Those were the days! My father and my husband, God rest their souls, didn't touch the stuff. It was your father who inherited the habit. He also enjoys a good drink."

I laughed along with her while I looked around the magic room. It was tiny, under the stairs, and had a wooden bench with a worn-out foam cushion covered with a faded red flowery sheet and a very old wooden desk with several books in English on it. There was nothing else in the room, and it was obvious that the old woman did not care about cleaning it daily like her God-rest-his-soul's room. Next to the magic room, adjacent to the staircase, was a small bathroom, which my great-grandfather must have installed in order to avoid walking all the way to the main bathroom.

I accompanied her to the kitchen. The women were busy at work: one washed the dishes, another stirred the contents of a big aluminum pot, which must have contained the soup made from the aforementioned duck, and another dried the dishes. Everyone was talking loudly and at the same time, though they quieted down a bit when the old woman entered the kitchen. Someone told her, "Go and rest, Grandma, we're nearly done." At this the old woman snapped, "I'm not dead yet! I still have my health." That was met by simultaneously murmured prayers for her health and long life. I sat on a wooden bench and watched the matriarch direct the women of the family: "Add some pepper to the soup. The duck is not crispy enough. The rice is fine, but cover it so it doesn't dry up. Which one of you stuffed these pigeons that are falling apart?"

A small kitten sneaked in, lured by the delicious smells. I don't like cats. No one in our family does. I got a towel, and was about to shoo the kitten away when Rawya gripped my hand and said sharply, "Leave her, Nadia. She'll leave of her own accord."

I was embarrassed. "Sorry, Ammeto. I didn't know you liked cats. It's just that I don't like them at all."

The woman stirring the soup said, "No one in this family likes cats, Nadia. You just don't know the full story, because you're not from here."

As another of the women was cautiously giving the cat some leftovers, I heard the full story that everyone else in the family knew. Once upon a time, a long time ago, a distant relative of ours, whose name was not mentioned for fear of bad luck, was in her kitchen when a fat black cat came in and snatched a chicken off the kitchen counter. Flustered, the woman lashed out at the cat with the big knife she was holding. The story goes that the cat was cut open without shedding a drop of blood. Then the kitchen filled with smoke and a hole opened in the floor, out of which a tall, dark woman appeared and, in a voice filled with pain, yelled, "Why did you kill me?"

I listened as the women took turns supplying the details of the story while they worked. One of them said that our relative then passed out, and when she awoke the cat was gone and all the kitchen utensils were scattered around on the floor. She remained unsettled for a long time, and rumor had it that whenever she entered a room things jumped around and fell to the floor, and that she spent the rest of her life in fear of the dark woman returning to punish her. Since that day, all the women in the family hated cats but treated them with utter respect and never shooed them away, by way of apology to the cat woman.

One of the men sitting with my father talked about his daughter and his wife, who was helping in the kitchen, stressing proudly that his daughter was getting the best education available and that he never denied her anything. "How old is your daughter, Mustafa?" asked my father, and Mustafa, still full of pride, replied, "She's ten, Uncle." He then called loudly to his wife. When she came out of the kitchen holding a towel, he reproached her with affected tenderness: "Haven't you done enough? Come sit with us and have a rest. Or will you spend the entire time on your feet every time we come here?"

I thought his attitude was pretentious and in bad taste—all the women were in the kitchen to help the old woman. Later my father would say that it was how some of the men in his family acted when they tried to appear cultured and progressive. He said that man probably considered his wife and kid to be part of his possessions, like a good shirt. He wanted them to look good in front of others, but couldn't care less when they were at home. He told me that when he was younger, relatives like this one—but from his generation—caused him a lot of anxiety: it seemed to be an inherited pattern and he used to fear he would find himself repeating it.

We finally all sat around the long dining room, the women having prepared the food and set the table; I had timidly helped with the final preparations. Conversation flowed, with the old woman at the head of the table, my father next to her, and me next to him. The food was delicious. I still remember the taste. I have traveled a lot and eaten in many places, but have never, before or since, experienced that taste. The pretentious man kept putting food into his wife's mouth with the same fake tenderness. His child was spoiled and annoying, talking in a loud voice and only stopping when the old woman gave her a look that would have shut *me* up! The old woman was both gentle and intimidating. She was a dominant presence and appeared to have control over everyone. But when she was out of earshot, the women would joke among themselves, "The old dear seems to have lost it."

By early evening, we were in the car and driving back to Cairo. My father glued his face to the window and watched the road again. I could feel that he was drained by the visit. He didn't say much, except to ask me if I'd had a nice day. I said yes, and agreed that we must visit the countryside every now and then and not stay away too long; that it was important to be present and keep our connection with the rest of the family so they wouldn't forget us. He replied that, yes, we definitely should visit again soon. But his tone told me that he knew this was going to be the last time.

19

ZAYN WAS EXACTLY FIFTY WHEN we met. I was twenty. He wrote poetry, and was sensitive and gentle and very attentive. He didn't look particularly old, he wasn't wrinkled or flabby, but he *was* fifty. Thirty years lay between us. The literature student who wore her hair in a bun and did nothing but glare at everyone—a temperamental, insolent bookworm was what everyone saw—fell in love with a poet thirty years her senior. It seemed a willful clinging to a cliché that would follow a predictable route and could only end one way. But Zayn was charming. He was sensitive and innocent, and I've always found the innocence of men hard to resist. I fell in love with Zayn, and he fell in love with me.

I don't remember the first time we met. Was it at a gathering at a downtown café? Or did we meet on a colorful sidewalk in Argentina while khaki tanks roamed the streets around us? Or was it in an American pub, where he spotted me among the late-night dancers? Or maybe we met by a waterfall in Zimbabwe as we watched the creatures of the wild make their way along the riverbank. Or on a beach in Essaouira, the sea endless before us. We could have met anywhere. All I know is that we had finally found each other and I didn't want us to ever part.

Zayn was an amazing human being, full of beautiful stories and sad poetry. We would sit together on the small sofa at his place, I resting my head on his thigh as he read me his poetry.

Standing on my balcony
On the calm weekend morning
I used to see her
Hanging her children's clothes
Her husband's yellow formality
His freshly washed white shirts
On lines of light and song
She radiated the purity of her content heart
As she came or went
Now after a bad summer
I see her
All withered eyes and limbs
Hanging black clothes on lines of silence and tears

I closed my eyes and whispered, "Zayn, could you talk about something other than death?" He kissed my head and recited softly:

When it is erected to block the sunrise
We might spend an entire lifetime
Drilling a hole so that light would

Just once
Reach a future generation
Without that wall
We would not have learned the value of escaped light

I turned to him and smiled. "By the way, Zayn, I love you." He hugged me and kissed my forehead. For a few moments, the universe stood still.

My relationship with Zayn was a happy one. I was in love and the complete happiness of it showed on my face all the time. I would meet him outside his house and we would stroll around the streets of Downtown. He would hold my hand and kiss it in the middle of the street. I was filled with pride and intoxicated by his touch. Sometimes I felt that I only loved Zayn because he was a poet and a dreamer. Our relationship was impossible, but I wanted nothing except to love him and be loved by him, and to hear him recite poetry and have him stroke my hand when I was tense or unhappy.

I couldn't keep our relationship from my father for too long. He sensed that there was someone in my life, so I decided to give him the details.

"Baba, he's not like anyone else. He's not like you, so don't even start on the clichés of looking for a father figure. That would be beneath me and beneath you, so don't go there. He's a nice man. He reads me poetry. He loves me all the time, not just some of the time. He is not like other men. I have found him and I will keep him, until I have had enough of him or he has had enough of me or something happens that breaks us apart. You should not find that difficult or ridiculous. This has nothing to do with daddy issues. I don't have any. I wasn't looking for an older man so I would find you in his shadow. Accept Zayn, or don't. He will stay until I decide that he goes, or he decides that I go."

My father was upset by my assertive speech, by my pre-judging his reaction without giving him a chance to speak. He looked at me without saying anything, and after a few minutes he said, "Whenever he decides to leave or you decide to make him leave, let me know. If you want, that is." I decided that I wasn't going to argue or sulk or slam my bedroom door like I used to as a teenager. I just said, "OK, I will," and gathered my things and walked away.

I went over to Zayn's. I put down my backpack, and took out my tobacco pouch and the small colorful lighter that Zayn gave me to get me to stop using matches. He didn't like the smell of matches and, although I did like it, I went along with his wish. I took off my jacket and folded it carefully and put it in my backpack. I walked over to Zayn, who was watching me from his place on the sofa, gave him a kiss on each cheek, and assumed my position with my head on his thigh and my legs dangling from the other side of the sofa.

"Zayn, I told my father."

"Have you heard a Fairuz song called 'He Brings Me Greetings'?"

"Zayn, I said that I told my father about us."

"OK. Why is that a problem?"

"It isn't. I'm just telling you."

"So have you heard the song I'm telling you about?"

"No."

"You know what it says?"

Love has come early to our quarters
Carrying stories and tears and joy
All the girls were gathered here
Mama, why did he choose me?

I smiled and put my hand in his. "Why did he choose me, Zayn?"

"Because you are you. You sparkle. No one will ever be able to cover you in dust."

Zayn's love grew in my heart. I planted my kisses on his face and engulfed him in my love. I would only spend a few hours at a time with him. I couldn't stay away from my father for too long. I would go to university, then to Zayn, then back home to my father. Even if we had been arguing, nothing was like settling next to my father at the end of each day, and resting my head next to his beating heart. It was the only place where I could put aside all my worries and tiredness, the stress of the streets, the lecture halls, the traffic—even Zayn's words would be temporarily forgotten while I enjoyed absolute and utter peace in my father's arms.

20

I TOOK A HEAVY COAT with me. I didn't have enough cash, so I decided to go to the airport, where I'd heard some cash machines still worked. I took the thick scarf that usually accompanied me on trips to colder places. I didn't take the small pocketknife that I had purchased from a fifteen-year-old boy and that I boasted about my ability to use. There were citizen-committee checkpoints everywhere and I wouldn't want it to get confiscated. I told my father that I was going out. "I woke up early and made some food: the vegetables you like and a chicken boiled without any salt or pepper, so it's fine for your blood pressure and allergies. There's also steamed rice, which you'll really like. I'm not sure if I'll be able to come back tonight, but I probably will. I don't want you to spend the night alone."

"OK. I won't be going out. But if you manage to come back in the middle of the day to update me on what's going on, do that. I'll be glued to the TV. Have the newspapers been delivered?"

"No, but forget the newspapers, there's nothing in them. Check Al Jazeera or anything that's not state TV, because that won't be showing much. I'll try to come back at some point in the afternoon."

"Take care of yourself."

"I will."

"Don't do anything stupid."

"I won't." I hugged him tightly.

I got a taxi to the airport, found a working cash machine, withdrew some money, and headed to Tahrir. The streets were empty. I felt a sudden twinge of fear. There was fear on the faces of the few people I saw. The long main road leading from the airport to Tahrir was almost empty except for the tanks and armored vehicles. They moved heavily through the city's streets and looked kind of ridiculous. It was an unfamiliar sight, and made me think of Chile during military rule. Not that I'd ever been to Chile, but I had seen pictures in history books. The taxi driver was nervous and kept murmuring to himself. "What are you going to Tahrir for?" he asked me. The question made me suspicious. He might be resentful of what was happening and take it out on me. So I replied, "I'm not going to Tahrir. I'm visiting a friend who lives near there."

"This is no time for visits," he said. "Haven't you seen what's happening? There are thugs all over the place. And you're a girl. You have no idea what we see on the road. You must be careful."

"God protect us," I whispered.

I got off at Qasr al-Nil Bridge. There was a big checkpoint at the entrance to the square—about fifteen young men and women checking IDs and searching people, with friendly but firm smiles. I let one of the women pat over my clothes, look inside my handbag, and peer into my face. I smiled, and she gave me the victory sign and said, "May God be with us." I nodded to her in approval and walked into the square.

I searched impatiently for Rima. On the first day I had seen her run to escape the tear gas, her long curly hair flying behind her as she leaped along the sidewalk, moving swiftly to avoid the tear gas canisters and rocks. I finally found her; her hair was a mess and her eyes were shining with enthusiasm. She hugged me. "Where have you been? I've been looking for you."

I replied calmly, "I only just got here. Baba is at my apartment, so I cooked for him, went to withdraw some cash, and came straight here."

"Come. Let's go sit over there for a while."

I walked beside her back to the entrance of the square, and we sat on the sidewalk. Months later, during the summer sit-in, the sidewalk would become our sanctuary. From this same spot we watched dozens of sunrises and sunsets. That day we sat in silence for a few minutes. I knew her pain. She'd always been a natural optimist. When she walked, it was as if she were flying. She exuded freedom, oscillated between joy and confusion, wrote down what she felt. All my memories from the square have Rima in them. We sat on that sidewalk and on countless others. I watched the square around me and started counting the faces. I gave up after a hundred.

"What's going on?" I asked Rima.

"I don't know." She sounded tired.

Every now and then the chants would pick up. There were dozens of street sellers. I noticed a wooden table on which woolen socks were laid out. I laughed. "Why is this man selling socks?" Rima replied seriously: "For the people camping here, Nadia. They can't all stay without changing their socks. The smell would end the sit-in!"

Armored vehicles and tanks blocked all the entrances. No one bothered us. The soldiers tried as much as possible to avoid friction. Some of the guys would pick up conversations with them, offering them cigarettes and bottles of cold water. Rima and I got up and went to a nearby bakery and bought a few dozen loaves of bread. At the store next to it, we got a box of water and some small cartons of juice. Some passersby offered to help us carry the bags, and we stood at the side of the square and started to give the stuff away. Within minutes the bags were emptied.

"What I would do for a Merit cigarette," I sighed to Rima.

She eyed me coldly. "Just smoke what we have, Nadia. This is not the time to be spoiled and demand imported cigarettes."

"I'm just saying," I said in irritation.

She pulled me off to go and find Layla and Galal.

The square was calm. Nothing signaled violence or clashes. The four of us gathered at the edge. Galal was disheveled, his shirt discolored by dirt. Layla was tense. We all talked over each other, trying to ascertain that everyone was OK.

I took Galal by the hand and told him nervously, "You know, of course, that you shouldn't leave the square. There are so many rumors flying about outside, and they've been arresting people on their way out."

He smiled reassuringly. "Don't worry, Nadia, I know. I'm not leaving any time soon. Let's just wait and see what happens."

As I looked at him, fear flooded my heart. I tried to appear calm, and at times felt that I was overreacting. Layla was nervous too, but she wasn't emitting as much negative energy as I was. Galal laughed and said, "We need to find some Valium for Nadia. What's the worst that could happen? So, they might arrest us. They might bomb the whole square. There's no way of knowing, but being anxious won't change anything."

"Weren't you just five days ago telling me that nothing at all would happen? 'It's just a demonstration, Nadia. Don't get your hopes up.'"

"You say that as if I or anyone could have predicted all these people turning up." He was visibly moved. I touched his shoulder.

I couldn't stop thinking about my father. I didn't want to leave him alone for too long. I would go to see him and maybe come back when he went to bed. I said good-bye to everyone and hugged Galal tightly. They all laughed and called me overdramatic, so I swore at them and took off.

21

My youngest aunt owned a small flower kiosk. She also designed silver jewelry, adorned necklaces and bracelets with colorful precious stones, and sold them to friends and relatives. She did many things, and she liked colors and strange designs. She had never married. Since my childhood, I had always seen her as the most beautiful woman in our family. She wore delicate clothes with lace details. She was in her fifties when she gave up everything else and bought a small kiosk, using the money of her share in the sale of my grandfather's land. There was no one to tend the land, but she could tend flowers. She read a lot about flowers, and began by growing chrysanthemums. I didn't know much about flowers except that I liked lilies. Any man I got close to soon discovered that a bouquet of lilies could put me in a good mood for at least a day.

But my aunt grew chrysanthemums, delicate flowers with pinkish petals and a dark yellow heart. The flower's name was beautiful, but it didn't do justice to its delicateness and sweetness. My aunt arranged flowers in vases and sprinkled them with cold water. She also grew daffodils, irises, tulips, and Egyptian red roses, which filled her kiosk with their fragrance—real roses, not like the odorless, spiritless ones I saw in the fancier flower shops. She sourced plant food from strange places, and asked anyone coming from abroad to bring her seeds so she could add new species to her beautiful, mesmerizing bouquets.

Zayn always brought me flowers. He used to go to my aunt's kiosk and buy me a bouquet of his favorites with a single branch of lilies with closed buds in the center. I'd receive this gift eagerly. In each flower I saw a word Zayn had told me in a moment of clarity. I placed the flowers in the big vase at his place and instructed him to sprinkle them every morning with cold water, until the lilies opened and their dark hearts leaped forward with a passion for life akin to my own in those days. I don't think I have ever been as open to life as I was when I was loved by Zayn.

I miss his words, his tenderness, the pleasure of feeling his hands on me. I remember my eagerness to taste life. I wasn't exhausted back then. I didn't wake up every morning dreading the start of a new day. I woke up at peace; no preemptive damning of the day to come, of which I knew nothing yet. I woke up early and raced through the day until the time I saw Zayn. He was good-natured, serene, understanding, mature, and just brilliant in every way. I wanted every new day to go on forever, because of Zayn and for him. With him I could be myself and no other. I could rest my body and my nerves. The scent of lilies penetrated my every cell. I closed my eyes and felt a deep calm—a sensation that I and everyone I loved were safe from illness and death. As Zayn read poetry to me, I entered a gentle trance.

> If only we were two branches of a tree
> Our veins fed together by the sun
> Drinking together the dawn's dew
> Turning together a buoyant green
> Standing tall and reaching out
> We dress in colors in the spring
> Shed our clothes in the fall
> Expose our naked bodies
> And in the winter, we bathe
> Kept warm by devotion

I slept in Zayn's arms with a smile on my face. Nothing that had come before or was still to come mattered then.

22

Ali was coming over for dinner. It had to be something new because I thought he must be bored with the usual. Though he used to say that I cooked with my soul, and once, when I was away on one of my long trips, he wrote to me: "Come back. I miss you and miss your cooking! Whatever you make turns out good!" Ali had a clumsy way of expressing his feelings sometimes, but I got him. I opened the freezer, got out some chicken breasts, and put them under hot running water. I had some potatoes and thought I could make mashed potatoes, which Ali liked. I would add some cheese. But I wasn't going to start yet. The day was still long.

I lit a cigarette and inhaled the smell of the burning match. I looked out of the window to the horizon and thought of Ali. He always came up behind me when I stood at this spot, putting his arms around me and resting his head on my shoulder, both of us looking out at the world. I'd smile—a smile he didn't see. Nothing mattered in those moments but the silence between us. I smiled at the memory, then frowned again. I always knew those moments were transient. He knew that too, but as usual he didn't seem to care.

"So what if I wake up one morning and feel I don't want to come to you any more? What's the big deal?" he would say.

"It's no big deal, Ali; it's just that endings are always kind of painful."

"Yeah, but what matters is that we'll always have this beautiful thing between us."

There was no point in trying to persuade a child that life wasn't that simple. Endings were painful and cruel and left permanent and bloody scars. If I had said any of that, he would have frowned and shut me out. I would have spent the rest of the day trying to make it up to him. It was better to let it be and leave endings to another day.

Ali always came over late in the evening, when he was done with his coffeehouse sessions with his friends whom I didn't know. I knew some of their names, but he was careful to keep his life a closed circle I couldn't enter. And I didn't ask. Mostly I didn't want to know. The solitude of my dimly lit studio was all I could handle at that point in my life. I'd had my share of searching for peace in people's faces and stories and only rarely finding it. I had the old places I used to visit, my own coffeehouses and hangouts, desolate and dreary now that most friends had dispersed—those who got married, those who left the country, and those who, like me, had had enough.

And so I didn't want to know what I didn't need to know.

Ali always came in the end. On the doorstep he would take me in his arms and hold me tightly, for five minutes, maybe ten. I no longer experienced time as I used to. We would eat together, maybe spend some time watching TV—I looking for news, he grabbing the remote to look for anything that was devoid of violence and disturbance. As we sat side by side on the sofa, he would take me in his arms again, maybe for an hour or two. Maybe less. I only noticed the time when the call to prayer rang out from the neighboring mosque, signaling daybreak. We were quiet for a few minutes before sleep, or sometimes we talked about random things. I could be talkative when I was in a good mood, and Ali liked to hear my stories and reflections.

I remembered our shared details and lost track of time. I watched cigarette ash drop to the floor and breathed in the unpleasant burning smell of the fourth cigarette filter, or was it the fifth? I turned on the TV to find Kamal al-Shinnawi holding Shadia and whispering in her ear, "Nawal, forget everything but this moment that we have together." I had watched this film so many times before, but it still always held my attention. The ashtray beside me slowly filled up. I empathized with Shadia, the cheating wife resisting the end of the affair with her lover. The same scene got me every time. Endings are the same in all their forms, but are especially painful when one side does not accept that it really is the end and gets stuck instead in an endless loop: final attempts, pleas, anger, repeat. The end is the end. I shivered at the thought. I put out my seventh cigarette and hugged myself, trying to expel all thoughts of leaving and dying. There wasn't much difference between the two. Leaving is a form of death for me. Every time someone I loved left, my subconscious translated that as a death. He was not coming back. Those who die do not come back. My brain buried them in a darkness akin to the grave. Those who leave do not come back.

The chicken was completely defrosted. I had to cook it before it went bad.

23

I KNEW ALI WELL. HE was like a child. When he listened to me, he was full of curiosity and passion, always wanting to know more. When I stopped, he begged me to finish the stories I had begun. I became his Scheherazade of sorts. A story was always required to keep him interested and happy, even if it made him nervous. Without stories, he found everything about our post-coffeehouse closeness boring—the dinner, the TV, and me. He didn't talk much, and when he did, his stories were no match for those of his sad Scheherazade. He was like a child asked which he loved more, his mom or a toy, and who replied with endearing enthusiasm, "I love the toy more because it's pretty and doesn't yell at me." He was clumsier and more tactless than a child; he would lie next to me and talk about boredom, and about his lack of feelings. He would go on about his sins and mistakes, occasionally blaming me, often making me so angry I had to get up and lock myself in the bathroom, behind the only closed door in my apartment. I cried a few tears then, before washing my face and rejoining him as if nothing had happened. When I did that, though, he became sensitive for a few days in order to avoid upsetting me or maybe to avoid the feelings of guilt that would follow him into his closed coffeehouse circle.

The streets remained unchanged. So did the ceiling of my room. And time. Time passed slowly and heavily, as if the hands of the clock were carving the numbers on my body. Death remained present too: in the kitchen knife, in the large window that tempted me to see the view upside down, in the delicate noose-like scarf I wore for warmth, in the speeding cars that I barely avoided, their drivers yelling at me in panic. Death was present in everything around me. I was scared of where those thoughts might lead me; my fear was of losing the bit of fear still left in me and one day finding in myself enough courage to follow those thoughts to the end.

Ali always came—sometimes he was days late, but he always came in the end. Sometimes I went away for long periods, other times we fought over trivial matters and didn't speak for a while, and sometimes we were just silent, but we always found each other again. And every time, there was the doorstep hug, which I never tired of.

On those days when Ali came and brought happiness with him, the food was delicious and the TV fun to watch, our bodies on the sofa merged into one, a fading sun shone through the large window. When he was in a good mood, I could see his very soul shine through his big, childlike eyes. On those days, he talked without fear or inhibition, or he shed his inhibitions as he talked, at peace with me and the whole world. Those days flew past with unbelievable smoothness, like hours stolen from time itself, spoiled by nothing but the moment of parting.

We held everything between us: dreams, warm moments of happiness, shared paths, and virtual universes; each other and what we used to be, many years ago; our life experiences, our friends and families, the bridges we tore down to eradicate all the distance that separated us, the faint yellow light of the room that saw our partings and encounters. There were white lilies between us, and a small colorful box that I had before me day and night in which we carefully placed our memories.

But there were also so many people between us, with no purpose but to watch us and impose their strange world on us, with its ways, words, habits, and pretenses; they pulled us into their coffeehouses and gatherings, and we lived in constant resistance. Between you and me, Ali, were your eyes, which I have run out of metaphors to describe. There was everything between us, but it all existed in a very tight space. There were no gaps or emptiness. Nowhere to move. We were held closely together by a strong glue that we had discovered and decided together to use, even while we knew that removing it would be painful as hell. Pain is a generic word, meaningless unless you've lived it. Pain was nothing compared to what we put each other through.

I could not compare this with what I had with Zayn: he was a safe haven. When I rested my head on Zayn's thigh, the world slowed down around me. That was a time before this smell of decay started to appear in my kitchen. These days I find strange things. There's a tiny spider that has made its home in my kitchen, so tiny that if I blink it disappears, only to reappear a few days later from behind the fridge. Now, the smell in my kitchen comes and goes. I look for its source, to no avail. Sometimes I find a moldy tomato or something left in a corner, but other times I find nothing at all, just the smell. Ali can't smell it. I've used all types of cleaners and disinfectants. Two or three times I saw a big cockroach crawling slowly and confidently across the kitchen's threshold. The last of those times, Ali was there and it made him jump, but then he killed it and threw it in the toilet. I looked at the dead cockroach and couldn't think where it could have come from. I live on a high floor in a tall building and there are no openings through which a cockroach could have crawled into my apartment.

In Zayn's days, there was just peace and poetry and our walks hand in hand in the streets of Downtown. I clung to Zayn. Now Ali was clinging to my clothes and waiting to get bored.

—

24

I SKYPED WITH RADWA AND told her what was happening. She told me that Ali was a child and that he would break my heart. I told her I knew. I could predict all of Ali's actions and was waiting for the day of the final heartbreak. I told her that I didn't know if I was happy or miserable. I just knew that I saw Ali's eyes everywhere—in the bathroom mirror while brushing my teeth, at the door. At every turn, his magic eyes were watching me go through my day. I remembered Zayn and cried a little. Radwa got upset and told me that I had become soft, not as strong as I used to be. "Where's the Nadia I know who used to simply shoo away half-men? He's not a full man, Nadia. Forget about him and take a breath. You got yourself into a difficult tangle. You know what? Just say bye. You know how to say bye?"

I laughed, feeling somewhat choked. "No, I can't say bye. I'll wait until he says it."

"Suit yourself," she said angrily. "Just keep torturing yourself until a vein pops out."

Radwa didn't know, when she used that expression, that I would wake up a couple of months after that chat with a strange bulge in my neck. When I looked in the mirror, there was a big, bulging, blood-red vein in my neck. I touched it and murmured to myself, "Careful what you wish for, dear Radwa."

Some days I woke up and found myself completely alone. Radwa was on the other side of the globe. Ali was never there in the first place. My mother was dead, but she too was never really there. Like Ali, her presence always crushed my own, but she only ever existed in a parallel universe.

My father. I would go to my father. On dark mornings like this, I went to my father. I called him.

"Good morning."

"What's wrong with your voice, Nadia?"

"Nothing. Just feeling glum. Do you want to get lunch?"

"OK. Come on by, and let's have lunch here in Heliopolis."

"Cool. I'll be there in a couple of hours. I'll get ready now, then be on my way."

I hung up, feeling that I still had someone to talk to or even sit quietly with.

I got dressed and took a taxi, and watched the road all the way as was my habit. We crossed the traffic-laden flyover. Warda sang on the radio.

As much
My love
As the many dark beautiful eyes in our land
I love you

Endless billboards—ghee, underwear, fashions for veiled women, ice cream. Warda sang on.

Neither time
Nor place
Could put our love in the past

Every night that passed without you near me
My soul, my eyes

We were finally close. So much had changed in Heliopolis. New Kamal, where we used to eat fruit salad when we were kids, had turned into a big shop for mobile-phone accessories. The stationery shop where I used to get the things I needed for school was now a fish seller's.

As much as all that's been ever said
Of love or patience
I love you
Years I spent awake
Singing your love

I got out of the taxi in front of the house and stood for a few minutes outside the big front garden. I didn't want to go in and see my aunts. Though I seldom cried, I felt close to tears and didn't want to end up crying in front of my aunts, who would be curious to know the reason. I stood in front of the house trying to decide what to do. I found my father sitting in his usual garden chair. He saw me and gestured to me to come in. I put my finger to my lips and signaled for him to come out through the garden gate. He laughed and disappeared inside the house for a few minutes, then came back out and opened the big iron gate.

He hugged me tightly. "Are you avoiding your aunts, you naughty girl?"

"I just can't face anyone. Let's go find somewhere to sit."

We walked arm in arm. My father was getting old. He didn't look it, but he was in his seventies, had a bad heart, and his breathing was irregular. Sometimes I woke up before dawn and found my breathing sounding just like my father's. We were prone to the same diseases: a weak heart and asthma. We were both chain smokers, or had been; he gave it up a few years ago, though he didn't mind a cigarette every now and then. But I smoked about forty a day. I enjoyed the burning sensation in my chest. He got upset whenever he saw me smoke. "All your arteries will get blocked and you will die. You'll see." To which I replied, laughing, "We will all die, Baba."

We walked slowly through the streets of Heliopolis, which still retained some of their old charm. An old woman who sold vegetables on the sidewalk smiled at my father and waved at him with a wrinkled hand. "How are you, Semsema?" he said good-humoredly. "You're looking beautiful today. When are you going to marry me?"

"The most beautiful morning to you, Professor. Behave, will you?" She giggled.

He laughed good-humoredly, then turned to me. "What's wrong, Nadia? Who's the son of a bitch making you sad?"

"Remember the guy I told you about? Ali?"

"Of course I do. The boy you're in love with. Did he turn out to be a jerk?"

I was annoyed. "Baba, don't trivialize things. I'm feeling seriously shitty, OK?"

He said, with the same tenderness I was used to since I was an infant, "Listen, Nadia, I told you ages ago: When you love a man, stay with him. If he's an asshole and you love him, stay with him. Whether he's a king or a beggar. If you love him, stay. When you stop loving him, leave. It's simple and uncomplicated. Do you love him or not?"

I hesitated. "Yes. I love him. Look, I don't know. I'm not sure."

"If you're not sure, then you don't love him. Do you remember when you told me about Zayn? How pissed off I was?"

"How could I forget? You wore a permanent frown whenever I saw you."

"Yes, because I knew you loved him. And I knew that you would have to leave him one day while you were still in love with him, or rather that he would leave you. Not because he was a bad man, but because of the circumstances. The thing that worried me and upset me most was that you really loved him. It was obvious. And your heartbreak was going to match that love. That's what I feared."

I looked at our feet as we walked. "Yes, Baba. I really loved Zayn—and I still do, by the way. But that's over and now I'm thinking about Ali."

"See—you can't even say that you love Ali."

"I need him."

"He's the one who needs you, you silly girl. Why do you do this to yourself, Nadia? Ali doesn't suit you. He's not mature enough. Zayn didn't suit you either. But he was too mature."

"Let's not bring age into it. It's lame. Also, those who live in glass houses shouldn't throw stones. I'm not saying anything."

He replied seriously: "I'm not talking about age. Nadia, you never go into anything with your eyes closed. But you're always worrying about others. You're always carrying the burden of some man. Why don't you find a man who carries *your* burden?"

"Really, Baba? It's as if you don't know me. I'd never be comfortable with a man who takes care of me."

He said sharply, "You only think so because you keep getting involved with half-men!"

I laughed. "That's exactly what Radwa said."

"OK, forget all that. What is it that's bothering you about Ali? Obviously you don't want to leave him, so what is the problem exactly? Is it something that can be fixed?"

His breathing started to sound labored. I pulled him into a nearby restaurant where we often had lunch. We sat in the outdoor area. I ordered a steak and he ordered steamed vegetables. I joked, "So which is better, this or the veggies I make?"

"Your food is better because you cook with your heart. They're just doing a job."

I went quiet for a moment, then said, "You know what the problem is? It's that I know he will leave me. I know he's not fully with me. I'm just a novelty that he's trying out. I know that, but I don't want to be the one who leaves first. I want him to experience life to the fullest. That's what he needs, and it's his right to need this."

My father smiled. "You have to stop acting like you're everyone's mother. The last person I saw you treat normally was Radwa. Other than her, you treat people like they were your children. Ali is not your child. Only he is responsible for his life experiences. You can't put yourself and your feelings at risk so he can grow up and become a man. That's just ridiculous. I'm telling you this will hurt you badly. And then I will have to kill him."

"Look at you, tough guy!" I laughed out loud. "No, I want him to have this experience. As you said, he doesn't suit me, but I don't want to leave him. Let him see this through, and I promise I'll try not to get too hurt."

He patted my hand and said, "Live your life, Nadia. Time flies and our lives pass by so fast. You must have heard this before, but it's real. We blink and find ourselves old. Live your life and don't let anyone imprison you in their issues."

"Yes, sir! Now let's eat before the food gets cold."

We finished our plates and went on with the day—another day on which I did not shed a tear.

25

RADWA ALWAYS HATED POLITICS. SHE only talked in the most cursory way about what was happening in the country. Of course we shared the same political beliefs, but she always thought it was futile.

"It's too messed up, Nadia," she would say. "There's no point in trying."

I used to find this "no point" declaration extremely annoying. I heard it from so many people around me. So many had views about the hopelessness of the situation, but from Radwa it made me feel like I personally had failed. Her bitterness pained me.

Galal was exactly the opposite. He was more politicized than me and Radwa. So was Rima. They both believed there was a point in trying; that of course there was a point in trying. Layla stayed on the fence, hesitant and confused. She wanted nothing to do with politics. She was the oldest of our group and the furthest from street politics. She just thought, "For my son's sake there must be hope. I can't accept that there isn't." As for me, I tended toward pessimism. When I thought about things rationally, I found myself on the same wavelength as Galal. I could see promising signs. But when I thought about "us" as examples of the people who live in this country, I found us lacking. We weren't able to see anything through. We and most of those around us in the square belonged to a social class that didn't really have to work for anything. I think that if we had done a survey of everyone in the square, we would have found that the majority had parents who had worked in the Gulf in the seventies, during the ugly days of open-door economic policies, only for the sake of returning with a small car, an apartment in the suburbs, and a few gadgets. We, their children, didn't have to work for anything. Our lives were a mediocre compromise. Our demands were a mediocre compromise. We were mediocre at our jobs. We were not at the top of the ladder, like the big shots that my father often included in the bastards category, but neither did we have to struggle to put food on the table like those who might as well be living on a different planet—those whom we discussed with compassion, then forgot as we smoked our imported cigarettes.

We did nothing with our hands. We didn't produce anything. Our achievements were limited, as were our ambitions. We never went hungry, and when our salaries were depleted toward the end of the month, we bought local cigarettes and ate at cheap curbside sandwich shops. Our entire lives were a mediocre compromise. So I didn't understand the secret behind this uprising—or perhaps I should say 'revolution,' to avoid being chastised by Galal. This was not how I imagined a revolution. I didn't think revolutions were started by those who had mediocre lives, but by those who had no lives to begin with. Maybe this revolution was the first exception.

I wasn't pessimistic so much as surprised. The exaggerated civility of the square; the sudden good manners that seemed to have mysteriously descended on the middle classes. Why weren't we—Layla, Rima, I, and other women—being harassed? Sexual harassment was a norm that, every day, men on the streets treated as an acquired right. All of a sudden a flood of good manners was sweeping everyone along. It was as if an invisible airplane were spraying the square with a magic potion that made people nice to each other and made men respect women. I received this with suspicion and apprehension. I heard other girls say, "Wow, the revolution is changing people for the better," and I replied, "I'm not convinced. After ten years or more of being groped in public transport and hounded by men in the street, I don't buy this manners-utopia thing." They'd look at me in disgust and pronounce me bleak and unable to see the good side of life.

I can't deny that through the two weeks of the sit-in, the square really maintained itself admirably. Men and women were constantly cleaning, and a high degree of organization reigned. There was a corner for everything: newspapers, bloggers, food and drink, making signs and posters, so many of which used the power of sarcasm to attack the regime.

There was a place for everyone. Layla, Rima, Galal, and I were almost always together. Galal left us at intervals to attend meetings and discussions, and when he returned he was sometimes quiet and downcast, but more often lively and optimistic. We sat in our place on the sidewalk and waited—I, despairingly, for the moment I anticipated when the military was going to attack and shoot us all dead; Rima and Layla for the fall of the regime; and Galal doing all he could to keep morale up.

There were so many rumors. Some were never verified even after the sit-in was over. Most revolved around stories of people being arrested as they left the square, military police cars that picked up demonstrators and took them in for interrogation. There was also the recurring rumor of trucks carrying state-hired thugs approaching the square. We would suddenly see people running toward one of the square's entrances and shouting, "Watch out! The thugs are coming!" But after the running and panic, nothing would happen. It was true, though, that many—not all—of those leaving the square were arrested, but the rumors were exaggerated. And in those days I decided to be an ostrich anyway, my head deep in the sand. Anything that I did not see, if I was asleep or away from the square, was not real. That was the easiest way to face the stress.

On the third day, my father decided that he would spend the night in the square. This made me anxious, because of his age and health. But arguing with him about it would have only stressed us both out. I scanned the square, looking for a relatively safe spot for both of us to settle for the night, and told my comrades that tonight was an emergency; my father was joining us and they all had to be ready to receive him. Galal reassured me with a pat on the back. Layla and Rima smiled. God help us!

My father had a victorious smile on his face all the way to the square. He didn't say a word, just looked out of the window of the taxi, and his smile got wider and wider. I fidgeted. I kept taking things out of my bag and putting them back in. I had brought a blanket and one of those airplane pillows. I couldn't carry an extra blanket, so I would use my coat. I had his medication, a bottle of water, and a small plastic container with low-salt cheese sandwiches in it. The kind of food being sold in the square would have raised his blood pressure.

Once in, we embarked on the customary tour around the peripheries, stopping whenever we met friends. He bumped into many of his friends that day, and every five minutes I would hear the same comment: "What are you doing here? What about your health?" To which he confidently replied, "I had to be here. After all those years, I couldn't possibly miss the revolution."

I took him by the arm and we circled the big central island. He paused every now and then to watch, from behind his glasses, the young people holding their signs. Many of the slogans were comical. There were very young children carried on their fathers' shoulders and shouting revolutionary chants in their childish voices. I generally don't like the idea of getting children involved in politics, but the square's children seemed different. We were all wondering how these children would grow up after having experienced a revolution. We walked around with big smiles on our faces. A band was playing Shaykh Imam songs on a makeshift stage. I motioned to my father to sit for a bit. We sat down together on the ground. I watched him out of the corner of my eye. He was looking steadily at the stage, his eyes not moving.

> Egypt is the suns rising from prisons
> The blossoming gardens in our blood

I saw his eyes tear up. He was probably being taken back in time, remembering the sixties when he may have sung the same song with his comrades at al-Wahat Prison. Perhaps he was told to stop singing by a prison guard and received a lashing or two if he refused. But this was a different place and a different time. He would not have been bitter or resentful because of the injustice he suffered or the years he spent in exile. He definitely wasn't begrudging these young people their revolution. It might have felt strange, but it wouldn't have made him bitter like it did for many of his generation. That night I was certain that my father was happy and expectant, like me and millions of others.

We lay down on the ground to sleep, he on the small blanket I had brought, I on my coat. I saw him close his eyes with a big smile on his face, directed at the sky. For the first time in years, I didn't hear the wheezing sound coming from his chest; nor did I worry about the irregular quivers of his heart.

26

I GOT UP EARLY TO COOK breakfast for Ali. When I was little, my father used to let the fuul beans soak in water from morning till sundown. After sunset he would go into the kitchen, dice one onion, two garlic cloves, and one tomato, and put everything with the fuul into its cooking pot, the qidra. He'd cover the ingredients with water and place the pot on low heat on the stove. I would sit close by so I could smell the aroma as it filled the house. Hours later, possibly around midnight, he would switch off the stove and empty the pot into a big bowl. The fuul had to be tasted, fresh from this complicated process, which at the time I thought was simple. My father handled the ingredients with the accuracy of a scientist—he would measure everything and tell me that one rogue milliliter could spoil the dish. He instilled in me a respect for the process of making fuul. We would sit together to dip baladi bread in a shared bowl of fuul, mixed with diced fresh tomatoes, corn oil, cumin, and maybe some crushed garlic. My father was also the one who taught me to add white cheese to fuul and mash it in with a fork. I thought everyone ate it like that, but years later discovered it was a custom that belonged only to us.

I never dared to slow-cook fuul at home. It was my father's territory and I couldn't compete. A packet of dried fuul has a permanent place in my kitchen cupboard, but I can never bring myself to use it.

I wondered what I should make for Ali's breakfast.

We usually got up together in the morning after a quick kiss and maybe a morning cuddle. When I heard the water in the shower, I knew that I had exactly twenty-five minutes. There was no time to think. I squeezed some orange juice and put the bread on the stove. I would time myself by putting one song on loop and listening to it five times until Ali finished his morning shower, by which point I would have put cheese on the table and quickly fried some eggs, adding tomatoes, green pepper, and lots of onion, which he really liked. Ali came out fully dressed, and I got the brush to brush his long hair. It was longer than mine then, especially after the haircut I had gotten, based on an ill-advised request from him. He drank the juice, ate quickly, put his shoes on, and went to stand by the door.

I went over to him and looked him over once, twice, three times. I pushed my hands inside his sleeves and pulled out the cuffs of his shirt, adjusted them, and smoothed the hem of his jacket. I looked at him again and gave him one last kiss. He gave me a hurried hug and left. As he closed the door of the elevator, I closed my front door. The song would be in its eighth and final loop.

My road takes me away from yours
I call to you, I love you

I turned it off and smoked my seventh cigarette, to start my day without him.

There was a lark living in the tree opposite my house. I heard it every morning, and sometimes at dusk. I could almost make out words in its song, of my own invention naturally. I liked that lark a lot. It was sad like Ali; maybe the story it recounted was Ali's. Both of them had soft and delicate voices. I never saw the lark, even when I stuck my entire upper body outside the window to try to locate it. Just as whenever I sought Ali out, I didn't find him. I knew he was there but I couldn't see or touch him. Sometimes I admitted to myself that I didn't really want to capture the lark or Ali. It was enough for me to hear the sad song floating to me from the tree. I could enjoy their presence, so near and yet so far.

27

ZAYN SET A HIGH BAR for my definition of love. His presence in my life was both exciting and grounding. I didn't think of beginnings and endings and the usual complications of relationships; I didn't think about the future. Zayn's existence gave me all the peace I needed, as well as all the madness. I sometimes went to sit with him at a downtown coffeehouse. I would be carrying my small bag, with my university books and papers.

"Read me a poem you like, Nadia. Something close to your heart."

I got flustered. Most of the poetry I liked back then was in English, and I didn't trust my ability to translate it. In the end I settled on Coleridge, from "The Ancient Mariner," an old favorite of mine.

> Ah! well a-day! what evil looks
> Had I from old and young!
> Instead of the cross, the Albatross
> About my neck was hung.

He listened to me with kindness, holding my hand in his. The sadness in Zayn's eyes was real. He had been sad since his wife died. They didn't have children and he never remarried. He told me he had waited for years, until we met; that his life had passed by while he waited for me. He said he knew that something was going to happen, that he would meet this girl, and that through her, life would bring him solace. My heart beat wildly as he held my hand and told me I was his sparkling girl, his muse, the unsuspecting weaver of his dreams. Zayn didn't want anything from me, except to love me. It was enough, and not just at that moment; as I later realized, his love was enough to last me for the rest of my life. Years later, I met Ali and fell in love with him. Then I met other men. My heart was broken more than once, but Zayn's love always saw me through those disappointments.

Galal too didn't love me like Zayn did. But I believed him in that moment. I just wasn't excited; Zayn had used up my capacity for excitement. I listened to Galal's poised words with a calm familiarity. I've always believed him. He was honest, a revolutionary, and was not like the others. He was not a liar or a fraud. And he was charming. We all loved Galal and needed him. He was like our collective child. Rima would ferociously defend him whenever I was angered by his occasionally childish behavior. Layla would say that he was foolish and reckless and that we must all look after him. Deep down I knew that each of us had some story with

Galal, but that we had long since left those stories behind in order to form our uncomplicated friendship circle.

I didn't know the details of the other stories, but I knew mine. I knew that Galal would find creative ways to make me feel like I was one of a kind, that there was no one like me and no one had ever gotten this close to his heart. I felt an intense happiness—that perhaps didn't always show on my face—whenever Galal told me that he loved me. I would listen to him talk about the struggles and honesty of the poor, and I'd believe him. I recognized these words, as they had been my father's since I was a child. I believed everything that Galal told me about the oppressed classes. During those moments when, lying on my back on the ground in the large square, I felt despair, I only had to steal a look at Galal's eyes and see the hope pouring out of them to feel reassured again.

He knew that we stood in the same corner, tuned to the same wavelength. I would be filled with enthusiasm when I heard his voice chanting. If his voice sounded downcast, I felt myself on the edge of depression. My feelings toward Galal were unusual and confusing. He told me he loved me and said the same to a dozen other women, and yet I believed him and never accused him of lying or being unfaithful. We never entered into a real relationship where we would share our feelings and lives, but there was plenty of unrestrained affection between us. Even years later, I knew that Galal never hoped for more than a kiss from me, and that I would always be satisfied with a warm hug that was our consolation for everything we did not accomplish.

28

Communication networks were finally back after a five-day shutdown. Networks were reopened following a cheap, emotionally manipulative presidential speech. Not everyone was manipulated, though. Immediately after the speech, the square exploded with anger and resentment, tinged with ridicule. The square was powered by an innate honesty that filtered out lies from facts. Leaving the square exposed you to frustration and despair. I sometimes felt that it fell beyond the realms of geography and history, even as it was closely bound to both. It was like a fictional chronotope in Bakhtin's sense: a standalone whole that, while influencing external events, is hardly affected by them.

When I listened to the presidential statement with Rima, Galal, and Layla from within the square, we felt nothing but anger. When I remember our reactions now, they appear to me almost exaggerated. Rima and I screamed, "All they do is lie! How could anyone believe this son of a bitch? They want to trick us!" After the statement, I decided to go home, where my father was waiting. I needed a hot shower and a few hours' sleep on my comfy sofa. I was utterly exhausted and had to rest. As soon as it was morning, I kissed Rima and Layla and Galal, and raced home.

My father received me with his usual enthusiasm. "Phones are back. Is yours working?"

"Yes, probably. I just need to charge it."

"What brought you home?" he asked apprehensively.

"Do you not want me back?" I joked.

"Looks like you got bored."

"Come on, Baba. I'm just tired and need a shower and some rest. I'll sleep for a couple of hours, then go back. Come with me if you want. I think it's safe."

I took all my clothes off and stuck them in the washing machine. I stood under the hot water and watched it turn black as it poured off me. There were layers of dirt on my body, and possibly insects too, as I found small bites in various places. It was perhaps the longest shower I'd ever had. I came out of the bathroom to find my father sitting in front of the TV. He seemed worried.

"Don't wake me up at all for at least three hours, OK? I really need a good sleep. Don't wake me up unless there's a disaster."

"I don't see how you'll manage to sleep."

"I'll manage, Baba. I'm callous like that. And if I don't sleep now, I won't be able to go back."

I almost passed out. Less than an hour later I was shaken awake.

"Nadia, Nadia! Wake up and see what's happening!"

Still in a sleepy trance, I said, "Baba, have mercy! Didn't I tell you to not wake me up?"

"Get up! There is a disaster happening as we speak. Come see what's on the TV."

I opened my eyes to an absurd scene on TV. For a few seconds I thought it was part of a dream, or rather a nightmare: a handful of camels and horses galloping through the square, while protestors tried to stop them from advancing. The riders pushed the animals on to run over protestors. There was a lot of screaming and blood.

"Who are they?" I yelled. "And how did they get into the square? Isn't the army guarding the entrances?"

My father answered bitterly: "What army? It's a conspiracy. The military tanks let them pass. It will turn into a massacre."

I started talking to myself, searching for my mobile phone. "Shit, shit, shit! Camels and horses? Has it come to that? What is this, the Middle Ages? They're attacking us with camels and horses, the sons of bitches!"

When I finally found my phone, I anxiously called Galal, who answered after the fourth ring. His voice was calm, but in the background I heard a fearful noise that sounded like drums, or banging on metal.

"Hi, Nadia. I'm fine, don't worry."

"What do you mean, fine? Don't lie to me! What's going on? Is anyone hurt?"

"No, my love, I'm telling you I'm fine. And Rima and Layla are fine too."

"OK, I'll get dressed and come over."

He replied hastily, "No, don't come now. Wait until things calm down. It's not safe now.

"I'm coming," I said sharply. "I'll call you when I'm on the way. Keep your phone on. What's that noise?"

"We're banging on the metal fences. To scare them away. So they'll think there are more of us."

I asked him to take care of himself and ended the call. To myself I murmured, "Don't die, Galal. Please don't die." I got dressed in a hurry and heard my father say, "Wait for an hour until things calm down. You won't be able to enter the square now at all."

I sat beside him in front of the TV. There were dozens, or perhaps hundreds, of people standing around the entrances and throwing rocks at the protestors on the other side. The military tanks were in the middle. There were almost no officers or soldiers to be seen. They hid inside their tanks and didn't interfere at all. With unbelievable callousness, they were letting a massacre happen before their eyes. The battle was getting ugly. The protestors managed to control the animals. At the same time, some of the thugs climbed to the tops of the buildings that surrounded the square and started to throw Molotov cocktails and firebombs down. All the while, the battle with rocks was continuing on the peripheries. Dozens of people were injured. TV channels transmitted what was happening live.

I heard my father's labored breathing and tried to reassure him. "Don't worry, things will soon calm down. Please think of your blood pressure. We have enough trouble as it is."

He regarded me in silence and then turned to follow the horror show on TV.

I called Galal again, but this time he didn't answer. I felt my chest tighten. I called Rima and Layla, but they didn't answer either. I was dressed and ready to go, but it would be impossible to get into the square now. It was surrounded from all sides. I had to go. There was no other way. I wasn't going to sit around feeling helpless.

My father's face went pale when, around seven p.m., I announced that I was going. I couldn't wait longer than that. He didn't try to stop me. "Take good care of yourself. If it's too dangerous, turn back, or go to one of your friends who live close to the square. Keep the phone on. I'll call you. Don't you dare not answer! If you don't answer, I'll think something's happened to you, and then you'll be sorry!"

"OK, OK! Don't worry."

I took off for the square. No taxis wanted to take me there. I decided to walk over from the direction of Qasr al-Nil. People I didn't know on the street waved to me to turn back. From a distance I saw thugs occupying Qasr al-Nil Bridge. I turned around and went through Abd al-Moneim Riyad, where I walked confidently among the thugs. I called Galal and told him I was nearing the Abd al-Moneim Riyad entrance. He screamed down the phone: "Have you lost your mind? You're coming from the worst direction! Go back if you can! Come through Qasr al-Aini." But before he finished, I had arrived at the armored vehicle that blocked the entrance. I saw strange things that hadn't been there when I left. There were metal barricades where the protestors stood. I turned my back on the unfriendly enemy lines and walked toward them. I was stopped by a young army officer who was covered in dust and looked exhausted. I thought I could make out a shoe print on his face, and I could definitely recognize a look of hysteria.

"What are you doing here?" he said in panic. "Where are you going?"

"I'm going to the square," I replied haughtily.

"The square? What world do you live in? There's a war in there, a war! If you try to go in, you'll get your head knocked off by a rock. And if you think I'll protect you, let me tell you, it's nothing to do with me. No one here is going to protect you."

"So what do you want me to do? I have to get in."

"I'll tell you what to do. Go and stand with those people behind you"—he pointed to a group chanting for the long life of the regime—"and start chanting with them. Because if they find out you're from inside the square, they'll eat you alive. That's the only thing you can do."

"Over my dead body! Fine, I'll get in through Champollion Street."

He gave up on me. "Do whatever you want. Just get away from here."

I turned back and started to walk toward the Champollion entrance to the square. Once again I tried to call Galal. I walked as fast as I could. Suddenly someone yelled, "Iraqis! Iraqis over there! Come on, guys!" I looked around and found a group of men heading in my direction. I didn't get it. What Iraqis? Where were they? Then I realized they were coming for me—that I was one of the "Iraqis." The next moment the back of my collar was in someone's fist. I was outraged, but before I could protest, they all started talking at the same time.

"I saw her talking on the phone. She has an Iraqi accent."

"She must be reporting back to whoever sent her here."

"I heard her with my own ears."

"I caught about four Iranians earlier."

"There are spies everywhere!"

"It's all because of those traitors inside the square."

I tried to explain that I wasn't Iraqi. I raised my voice to let them hear my Egyptian accent. But my naive attempts got me nowhere. They were hell-bent. I was finally saved by a taxi driver who appeared like a guardian angel. He stuck his head out of the window and shouted, "What did she do, guys?"

"She's one of the traitors from inside. She's a spy."

He raised his voice. "Oh, then we must turn her in! No need to beat her up. Let's do the right thing and hand her over to the army."

He motioned to me surreptitiously to get into the car. My captor's fist had loosened a bit on my collar while he talked to the driver. I slipped away and jumped into the taxi, which drove off immediately before they gathered that the driver was helping me escape.

I burst into tears the moment I got into the car. The driver looked at me in the mirror. He couldn't have been older than twenty-five. He said sympathetically, "Don't cry, miss. It's not worth it. If you make yourself ill, do you think this country will help you? It won't. And nothing's more important than your health. Take it easy, please."

He drove away from the square. I kept repeating, between sobs, "There's no point in anything, no point at all." Still regarding me in the mirror, he said, "Of course there is, miss! Don't you give up! You were just in the wrong place. You know what, I go to the square every day. I don't stay the whole day, but I go and see what I can help with—medication, cigarettes. I set aside thirty pounds every day to bring stuff to the kids who spend the night. It's not much, but every little bit helps, right? There's hope, miss. Those people who wanted to beat you up are just slaves to those in power. They've been brainwashed."

I said through my tears, "Don't call them slaves. They were probably paid to break up the square."

He replied in the tone of one in the know: "No, you don't get it. Those folks care nothing for money. They just get a kick out of this. They can't live without being under someone's whip."

His views on things disturbed me. I remembered Galal's words: "There's no such thing as a nation of slaves. Anyone who says so is a jerk. People might be poor but they aren't slaves."

I asked the driver, "Where are you going?"

"I'll take you home. Where do you live?"

"I don't want to go home. Please take me back to the square."

He exhaled. "And then what? What if they catch you again? Go home, miss, until things calm down. All hell is breaking loose in the square right now. The battle is at its height."

I said stubbornly, "Please. Just take me back to the square. Not through Abd al-Moneim Riyad this time. Take me through Qasr al-Aini."

"OK," he said, giving in. "Let's just try to find a safe entrance."

I called Galal. He could hear the tears in my voice. "Are you OK?" he asked. "Did anything happen to you?"

"I'm fine," I replied. "Where are you?"

"Come to Qasr al-Aini. I'm here with Rima and Layla."

The street was calm, though the pavements on both sides were all broken up. There were strange-looking types in Talaat Harb Square. The driver pulled up before we got to the first checkpoint. "It's safe here," he said. "Take my number. Call me if you or your friends need anything. I can get through anything. Just call. My name's Mansur. If you ever need anything, call me and I'll be there."

"I'm Nadia, Mansur." I smiled. "I don't know how to thank you. May God protect you."

"May victory be with us, Miss Nadia."

Mansur went on his way. I found Galal waiting for me at the entry point to the square. His shirt was torn. Rima had a dark look on her face and Layla seemed very anxious. I started crying again in Galal's arms. I told him in broken fragments what had happened, my head resting on his shoulder. Finally he moved me away from his shoulder and said, "Aren't you OK now? What's all this fuss you're making? Don't you know what's been happening?"

I frowned. "You think it was nothing to be captured by a mob shouting 'Iraqis'? They meant that I'm a spy."

"No, sweetie," he said. "It's not nothing. But we were running from camels and horses a few hours ago. We've had Molotov cocktails flying over our heads for hours. Rima was attacked. The thugs cornered her by a small shop, and if the shopkeeper hadn't stood up for her, they would have eaten her alive. Layla has been running around worrying about us all day. We're all in a state, I mean. So calm down and try to pull yourself together."

I went quiet, suddenly realizing how dramatic I was being. Galal added: "Also, *Iraqi*? You couldn't look more Egyptian."

"Well, Iraqis look like us," I murmured, then looked at Rima. "What happened to you?"

"I lived through a fucking horror movie."

Impersonating Galal, I pretended to make light of things: "Aren't you OK now? What's all this fuss you're making?"

We all laughed and some of the tension dissipated.

"Let's sit for a bit and take a break from all this," said Layla.

"You go. I have to get back to the front," said Galal, and started running in the direction of the square.

"Is Galal going to war?" I asked. "The front?"

"Oh, it's because you're a foreigner now. Let me explain," said Layla. "The square turned into a war zone in the past few hours. We now have, God bless us, the Champollion front, Muhammad Mahmud front, Qasr al-Nil front, and this one, Qasr al-Aini front. There are barriers and barricades and makeshift trenches on each one. They attack and we respond from our side. But inside the square it's also not entirely safe. There are people on top of buildings throwing Molotovs. We've been having a shitty time. May this day come to an end."

"But how do we know these are paid thugs?" I wondered aloud. "Couldn't they just be people who bought yesterday's bullshit speech? Guys, people outside really think that we're spies and traitors."

Rima shot me a ferocious look. "What's wrong with you, Nadia? You've seen for yourself. No one here has any weapons. They've attacked us on camel and horseback! And that squad on the roofs is throwing fireballs onto the heads of unarmed people. I have no idea what's happening outside, but we've witnessed a massacre here today."

"So what are we supposed to do now?" I asked, exhausted.

"Nothing," said Layla. "We wait till Galal returns. It's difficult to get into the square now. But when they start attacking from Talaat Harb, we'll try to move to a safer spot."

I'd completely forgotten about calling my father. I dialed his number and he picked up immediately. I told him calmly that I was fine and that where I was standing it was safe. I said that everything was going well, that the protestors had the situation under control.

Later, when I walked into the square, I could smell blood. Dozens of men and youths had their heads bandaged, the blood seeping through the basic cotton and gauze they'd used. There was blood everywhere. I started to panic. I hadn't imagined things to be this bad. Where had all this come from? The regime was trying to save itself through whatever means it could, crushing the dreamers in its way. For me, everyone in that square was a dreamer—people dreaming that by sheer will, they could change something so powerful, solid, and deep-rooted. In a country like ours, this was a wild dream, especially when it grew out of the middle classes. We were all cogs in the machinery of this immense nightmare. We produced nothing, only consumed and went around in circles. We had never experienced hunger. There are people in the world who commit or contemplate murder in order to eat or feed their children—those are the people that make revolutions. But there were not many of those in the square. We were mostly just dreamers . . . willful dreamers.

*

It was a black night. That's the only way I can describe it. On the Abd al-Moneim Riyad, Champollion, and Qasr al-Nil fronts, the violence didn't abate. On Qasr al-Aini, it stopped and started. The groups fighting on the inside defended the entrances ferociously. Galal came and went, returning to us for a few minutes, then leaving again. One time he came back with a head injury. He wasn't bleeding, but he had a big bump on his forehead and held his head in pain. But that didn't stop him from running back to the front.

I called my father at short intervals, every hour or two, to joke with him and reassure him that we had the square under control. He was panicking because of the news he was watching on TV, but hearing that I was fine calmed him down.

I didn't subject myself to any violent confrontations that night. I knew my limits. Nothing terrified me more than those rocks flying around. I couldn't bring myself to pick up a rock and throw it at another person, or even throw it into the air. It was then that I discovered I was a coward. I couldn't partake in the violence, which I viewed with awe and fear. I understood the position of self-defense in the context of a battle like this. Let the fighters fight. The most I could do was be present. I was just a body to add to the numbers of protestors. I couldn't contribute anything more than this. Or that's what I thought. Until I found myself a few hours later holding a hose and helping someone fill Molotov bottles with fuel.

I was in a trance and couldn't object. The young man who requested my help looked poor and would have been called a thug by the TV news, but he was on our side. I was leaning on a parked motorbike when he came to me, out of breath, his head in a bandage like most men in the square, and carrying an empty bottle. He said in a worn-out voice, "Hey, miss, hold this bottle for a minute."

I automatically did what he asked. He proceeded to open the motorbike's tank and insert a primitive hose into it. "Now give me the bottle, and hold the hose like this."

"Right, yes," I said in blind obedience.

I held the hose while he tilted the bike at a certain angle until drops of fuel started to trickle into the bottle. A few seconds passed before I understood what I was doing. What if this bottle killed someone, which wasn't at all unlikely? In the seconds that followed, I contemplated dropping the hose and running away. But I didn't. I waited until he was done. He took the hose from my hand, closed the tank, and said as he rushed away, "Thanks, miss. We'll be victorious, God willing!"

I murmured under my breath, "You're welcome, buddy. You and whoever will be hit by this."

It was unequivocally the longest night of my life. The night wouldn't end and the violence wouldn't stop. The sound of banging on the metal fences grated on my nerves. The battle continued till daybreak. We were continuously calling our friends to check if they were still alive. No one came out of the battle intact. We were all casualties in one way or another. Some were injured by bricks, others were traumatized by what they had seen or experienced, some lost their eyes, and then there were those who lost their lives. Things got calmer on the second day, and by daybreak the protestors were winning. The others were finally beginning to retreat, overcome by courage and numbers, and above all by determination. I do think that battle affected, on a personal level, everyone who took part in it. If you've witnessed so much violence and blood and fought for your own survival, it would be impossible to stay the same. Something changed in each one of us. My fear of violence increased, but also my support of its necessity in the face of overwhelming force. We all became more determined to carry on, and above all to maintain our sense of humor.

I heard someone recount to his friend how difficult it was to lead the captured camel down the steps of the metro station. "The camel gave us such a hard time!" I cracked up, just imagining the scene: the revolutionaries leading a camel down the steps of the underground metro station, which was used as a makeshift prison for those thugs they could detain. There was much debate in the square as to what they should do with the camel—slaughter it or hand it over to the army? Some said we should slaughter it, grill its meat, and eat it. Others thought that would fill the square with more blood, and we already had enough. The final verdict was to hand it over to the army, ending one of the most absurd discussions I've ever heard in my life. Revolutionaries discussing the fate of a captive camel, as they adorned lampposts with horse reins that were jokingly referred to as the spoils of war. The kind of absurdity you'd be hard pressed to find anywhere but in Egypt.

But the battle did finally end. The phase of counting losses that followed was painful. Hundreds of people died that day. Hundreds or maybe thousands were injured. People lost eyes, and some lost their sight altogether. The losses were huge. Still, the spirit of the square was like a magic balm over these wounds. The square was mighty and clear: it had power and influence and spirit. It supported and healed. It had a face and a voice. With unbelievable continuity it pushed us to carry through what we were doing. It left us no room for retreat or disappointment. Further proof was the state of people outside the square—breakdowns and despair. Few managed to maintain the same spirit outside the square.

Tahrir continued to attract large numbers every day, even if most went home at night. They returned in the mornings, afternoons, evenings, injecting enthusiasm and persistence into the protestors who were sleeping there. There was no explanation for this except that the square itself was pushing us forward. The powerful monster of the ruling authorities shrank a little more every day before the spectacle and the purpose of the square.

29

Ali came over with other friends. I sat on the rocking chair and he perched next to me. I tapped my foot nervously. All eyes were on us. He casually extended his arm behind my back and stroked my shoulder. The others were talking loudly. Gradually the voices faded, leaving the two of us engulfed in our silence. Only silence brought us together. I looked at Ali's hand and touched it for a second. It was warm. When the last person had left, he rested his head on my shoulder and slept.

This was what often happened when Ali came over with the others. He'd touch me coyly, suppressing the urge to throw himself into my arms. I knew that and saw it all the time. Ali belonged in my arms. He was like a cat. I would stroke his head and let him bury his head in my chest until he fell asleep. Sometimes, in his sleep, he would turn his back to me and continue sleeping with his face to the other side of sofa. But in order to fall asleep in the first place, he had to bury his head in my chest. I remembered my father's advice about not treating Ali like he was my child. I'd never been a mother and knew little about maternal feelings; I just responded to Ali based on how I felt. When he wanted to hide in my arms, I held him. When he wanted to go away and never come back, I left him alone and didn't call him.

Did I ever do anything that upset Ali? I must have. There were the days I would leave him and go to my wailing wall—in the big bathroom—then come back with puffy eyes and no explanation. He hated that. He wanted me to smile. And he wanted me to talk because he couldn't. But even on days when I couldn't smile at Ali, I would still look into his eyes to make sure the magic world still lived there. He didn't know how I saw him, and I—naturally—didn't know how he saw me. But in his eyes, I still saw all the lands I'd ever wanted to visit, all the innocence of an unspoiled world. I saw everything that was unattainable in this life.

I remember that time we went on a desert trip with our friends. There were about ten of us in a big tent and, as usual, they were all talking nonstop. I left the loud laughter and the many stories and slipped away to the void outside. At the door of the tent lay an infinity I knew well. I lay down on the soft sand, trying to sink down to its deepest layer, and looked at the sky. Since I was a child I had been looking at the sky. I looked for the three aligned stars. I'm not sure where I got the idea but I believed those three stars brought me luck and love. I always found them, but luck and love never found me.

The sky was so full of stars that night, and that time I couldn't locate my three stars. But I saw a meteor shower, ten or so shooting stars, and at the same moment Ali came out of the tent and walked over lightly to join me. He placed his arm under my head and looked up, searching for what I was looking at. I turned to him. He lay as if he were floating above the sand. He didn't sink like I did. I planted a kiss on his cheek. He smiled. A few minutes later he got up and set off running. I heard his laughter and sank deeper into the sand. Maybe it was on that night that I realized he was never going to be with me. I was inside the sand, sinking to the deepest possible layer, while he ran above it, his feet barely touching the ground.

Ali didn't remember most of what happened between us. His memory was selective. I sometimes thought that he forgot things intentionally to protect himself from hurting when we eventually stopped seeing each other. But I insisted on reminding him of the moments we shared. I too had a selective memory, and I was *choosing* not to forget. What he didn't know was that I loved him mainly so I could remember him when he was gone. If parting was always an unspoken presence between us, then let us save what we can. The memories would be all that was left when everything else was over. I would wait until his head was settled on my chest before sleep and start to quietly recount the moments we shared.

Do you remember, Ali, when I went to see Radwa, in the cold faraway country? I used all the communication tools of the twenty-first century to reach you, and you didn't answer. Suddenly you had stopped taking my calls. I sat in a beautiful room where the sun shone through the winter snow, and couldn't sleep. Long hours watching night turn into day and not sleeping. Do you remember, Ali, when you then suddenly reappeared in a text message to tell me that you were ill? Do you remember the exact moment when you told me that everything had gone suddenly dark around you and that I, sitting here thousands of miles away, was the last thing you thought of before the world faded away? I sat in that faraway room with my heart beating. I knew then that nothing mattered but you.

You didn't remember the moments we had, Ali, while I chose to forget everything else and remember my moments with you.

30

Things quieted down in the square. Two days had passed since the big battle. The protestors' good humor was on the rise. There were nights of singing till morning. We made our beds on the sidewalk, I wrapped in my heavy coat to avoid using the blankets with their gas smell and their fleas, while Galal would wrap himself up in a filthy blanket and sleep like he was lying in the most comfortable bedroom. His easy sleep annoyed me, so I decided to punish him: "Galal! Galal! Wake up, I need to talk to you!"

"Shut up, Nadia, and let me sleep."

"Galal, Galal, Galal, get up!"

He finally sat up angrily and said, "What do you want, Nadia?"

Acting like a spoiled brat, which was entirely inappropriate, I said, "I'm cold. I can't sleep."

"Cover yourself with a blanket and you'll be able to sleep."

"The blankets aren't clean. They're infested," I said coldly.

"Do you think you're at the Hilton? You're sleeping in the street. Cut the attitude and sleep."

"Galal, please get up and let's go for a walk. I'm fed up. Please come with me."

Our voices woke Layla, who said, "Just settle down and sleep, everybody! You woke me up. Nadia, take a blanket and sleep and let's just get through the night, please."

"I won't sleep. If no one gets up to go for a walk with me, I'll keep waking you up every time you fall asleep," I said stubbornly.

Finally Galal relented and stood up and pulled me by the arm. "Come on, then. You'd think we were on the beach. You want to go for a walk. You do realize we're in the middle of a revolution?"

As I walked triumphantly away with him, I heard Layla murmur, "Good riddance!"

We walked around the square. The dawn prayer hadn't been called yet. I watched the many tents on the traffic island in the middle of the square. Most protestors were asleep after another tiring day. But there was light in the field hospital by the Mugamma building, and a few young people sat in a circle by it. The oldest must have been twenty. I pulled Galal in their direction. We stood at a distance and listened to them sing old Muhammad Munir songs. I started humming along, then suggested we join them.

They welcomed us and sang with rising enthusiasm. I looked at their faces and smiled. When I was a teenager, I was a temperamental, unfriendly girl. I had my headphones on all the time and never sang aloud. I was difficult to get along with and would never have welcomed strangers into a circle like this one. I used to practice scowling in the mirror, ready to repel anyone who dared to come close. I watched these kids and smiled spontaneously. My heart beat in tenderness toward them. I thought they would never have to deal with bitterness like me, or fear like Layla, or uncertainty like Rima. Only Galal resembled them. He would still have his fresh-faced spirit when he was seventy years old. Galal was born with a cheekiness, a spontaneity, and a youthful sense of hope that would always stay with him. That was what I loved about Galal: his faith, his enthusiasm, and his excitement about life were intact.

I looked at his tired face, laughing and singing with the kids, and envied his faith and his clarity. I didn't know what to do, so I reached for his hand, and he spontaneously squeezed mine back, all the while singing and swaying his head with the tune. I left the singing circle and walked around the square. At every entrance there was a checkpoint. Familiar faces called "good morning" to me, and I smiled and answered. I stood watching a group of soldiers washing a tank at one of the entrances. There was a deep container with some cleaning liquid or solvent. Each soldier would dip a filthy rag into the liquid, squeeze it, and use it to rub one part of the tank. They did that every morning. The tanks would be covered with revolutionary graffiti and obscene curses directed at the regime, which would have angered their senior officers. So at the start of each day, before their superiors woke up, the soldiers would clean the tanks, which would just acquire new writings and drawings in the course of the day, while the soldiers looked on in frustration and prepared themselves to clean them again the next morning. As I walked past I called to them, "Don't clean so diligently. They won't stay clean." Time passed. Galal must have gone back to sleep.

I called my father. "Morning. Do you want to come here or shall I come home?"

"No, I'm coming to you. Wait for me at the Qasr al-Nil entrance," he replied quickly.

I laughed. "You obviously can't wait to be here! OK, call me when you're close. Let's have breakfast together."

I bought fuul and falafel sandwiches, then went to the field hospital to ask for an indigestion tablet to take after breakfast. My colon was acting up, and without the tablet I'd be sick all day.

Twenty minutes later, I met my father at the Qasr al-Nil entrance. He immediately started to explore the square with his eyes. He said the numbers weren't as high as the first few days of the sit-in.

"Don't be greedy," I joked. "Do you not remember the protests you used to drag me to, where all of you together didn't make up a hundred? Now you don't like that we're six hundred thousand instead of a full million?"

"I'm not complaining," he replied. "But the truth is it's the large numbers that will protect you from violence."

He led me in the direction of Bab al-Luq. He looked at the soldiers and officers standing by the armored vehicle at the entrance. We circled around and around it.

"Are we done yet?" I asked impatiently.

"Yes. Let's go to the Champollion entrance," he said enthusiastically.

I looked to him without understanding, but I went along. At Champollion, we did the same circling of the tank that blocked the entrance there. I finally asked, "What is it? Why are you circling the tanks?"

"I don't know," he said. "I just want to know what the military wants. They're not here to protect you. Don't believe that bullshit. If they wanted to prevent deaths, they would have protected you when the horses broke in. So I just don't get why they're stationed here."

"But what will our endless circling of them achieve?"

"I just feel that maybe if I have a close look at them I'd be able to tell. But my gut tells me that the soldiers and officers standing here don't really understand much themselves. I'm not sure, but I'm worried. The excessive military presence worries me. Take it from me: Military presence is always a cause for worry. Even if they do nothing at first. Be wary of them. Don't think that you and your friends are safe because they're here. One the contrary, they could be a source of danger."

"Don't be paranoid," I said flippantly. "The military worries me too, but there's no sense in panic. They've been sitting here since the last battle and they haven't harmed us in any way."

"But eventually they will," he replied confidently. "They won't shoot you out of tanks. That they wouldn't do. But they can give you trouble. Numbers must stay high. Otherwise it's dangerous."

We walked around the square and continued to circle the tanks and armored vehicles. My father watched the soldiers intently.

The square was not under threat at that time. Numbers were in the tens of thousands, and there were days when they didn't even reach a hundred thousand—at peak times, but these were still large numbers. A lot of politics was happening outside the square, and very little within it: the removal of the regime was the top priority. But outside, politicians met, committees gathered, conferences were held, and countless analysts and experts and officials and strategists attempted to design countless plans to end the political stalemate. All that was happening, while the square whistled along lightheartedly: Do whatever you like, we're staying until the fall of the dictator. None of us was really interested in the politics taking place outside. The square stood with us: prayers and songs and symbolic coffins, jokes and posters, all with a single aim. There was no leaving, whatever the politicians and masters outside decided.

31

Ten years have passed since I last saw Zayn. My feet still sometimes carry me toward the building where he used to work. I would find myself on the steps leading to his office, and catch myself at the last minute. I miss Zayn. Ten years have passed and I still miss him. I want to lay my head in his lap and sleep. For ten years I've been passing his building, and can almost smell him and see his shadow. I wait for him to come out to take my hand. I long to walk with him like we used to, with no particular destination.

I found out from my father. I was at university when he called and asked me to come home immediately. I rushed home with a quivering heart. I had a morbid feeling. Someone had called our home phone and told my father. It threw him; he didn't want to be the bearer of such sad news. But he had to tell me. I could smell death—I was an expert. Like a cat, I could sense death before it happened. Something was lodged in my chest and squeezing my heart. I couldn't breathe properly. Blood rose to my head, and I could feel its heat in my ears. I listened to what my father had to say. Zayn was dead.

My head felt like it was stuck in a concrete cast. A violent hammering filled my body. I went to my room. I wasn't crying. I started to hit my head on the wardrobe in rhythm with the hammering inside my body. A massive shiver went through me. Where was this chill coming from? I pushed the wardrobe closed with my head and stared at the dark wood.

What did it mean that he was dead? People didn't just die like that. I glimpsed my father crying. He wasn't mourning Zayn; he was mourning me and his own helplessness. For the first time in my life I felt totally lost.

I was in shock for a few months. I discovered that I found the idea of death difficult to grasp. My father gave me sleeping pills. I would wake up and find my face wet with tears. Until I lost Zayn, I didn't know that people could cry in their sleep. And my tears do not come easily. But in my sleep, they flowed freely, fresh on my face every time I woke up. My father insisted that I sleep next to him. I could feel him check my pulse in the middle of the night, making sure I didn't die of grief. I don't know if this was extreme, or if it was my grief for Zayn that was extreme. For the first time in my life, I felt betrayed. When my mom died, I felt ordinary sadness, and as usual I didn't cry. I didn't experience that sense of betrayal until I lost Zayn.

Radwa accompanied me to the wake. I managed to hold myself together. I wore black and sat quietly, not saying a word, except—as I remember—when I asked Radwa that we leave the large, eerily quiet marquee where the wake was held.

I found myself looking at the faces of other mourners and secretly wishing they were all dead instead of Zayn. When I went out into the street with Radwa, I started telling her disjointed things about Zayn, about the time we'd spent together and how I would spend the rest of my life in fear. Radwa remembers that day and says she had never seen me in that state of helpless panic. Zayn's death made me feel more panic than grief. I said to Radwa that he wasn't an old man—how could he die when he wasn't an old man? How could he die when he wasn't even ill? Radwa replied that people die for no reason all the time, suddenly and unjustifiably. She said I had to pull myself together for my father's sake.

"I'm scared," I said.

"There's no reason to be scared," she replied. "Just cry, Nadia. Crying will make you feel better."

We were young then. We hadn't gotten used to losing loved ones. We didn't know how to deal with death. And because we were young, panic was the appropriate response. Real sadness came years later, when it all sank in.

When I got home after the wake, I went straight to the kitchen. I took out some vegetables and rock-hard cubes of meat from the freezer. I put the bags of frozen food under the hot tap and stood staring at them, feeling a spray of hot water on my arms and face. I stood there for half an hour, maybe longer, without moving. Finally, I touched the cubes of meat and found them a bit softer. I peeled a large onion and let the stinging tears flow. I cut the onion slowly, then put it in the copper pot, added some butter, and stood quietly in front of the stove. I recalled my moments with Zayn—his tenderness, his soft words, and how I had begged him to stop talking about death. I remembered the melancholy of his poetry; remembered him laughing at my reaction and stroking my hand. He insisted on reciting the sad words into my ear. I would object and try to get up but he held me gently and read:

I asked you to want me, as you would want the season of fall
Or a river
I asked you to cross the river as if you were me, on my own
And to spread across the fields alone, as if we were together
I asked you to be
And not to be
I asked you to want me
As you would want the fall
To wither in you
Before we grow together
I asked you to want me
As you would want a river
And let me lose my memory in the fall
Before we walk together
In everything that we are
United by what keeps us apart

I burned the onion and let the meat go yellow under the hot water. I stood helpless before the stove: my hands felt paralyzed and I couldn't even lift the pot. I don't know how much time passed like this, but it was enough for everything to be ruined. I threw it all away—the meat and onion and pale vegetables. I stared at the mixture in the large garbage can, then went to bed.

32

ANOTHER DAY IN THE SQUARE that I pronounced miserable the moment I opened my eyes. I wished I'd just died in my sleep, because whatever we did, "there's no point in anything."

Galal sighed and said, "Oh, the gloom is starting early today. Good morning, Nadia."

I rubbed my eyes. "And what would make it good? Eighteen days have passed since all this started, Galal. You've been telling me for eighteen days that this is a revolution and that everything will be fine. There's no point! Stop being so stubborn and admit it."

Rima and Layla exchanged glances. Galal helped me to my feet and announced he would take me for a morning tour. I hung my head dejectedly and let him lead me by the hand around the traffic island. For a while he talked and I listened.

"You know, Nadia, we've been sleeping here for two weeks. You've been coming and going. Rima and Layla too. Lots of people come and go. But there are people who haven't left at all. They have been in the square the whole time. That determination is so strange. People could have left when the army was deployed, or when the square got attacked and they saw death close up. They could have left when numbers and hope dwindled, when 'sightseers' started visiting the square like they were visiting the zoo. You know? They could have left when the media started to disown them, called them traitors and mercenaries. They could have left many times over. But do you know, my dear Nadia, why they haven't left?"

I looked at my shoes, whose color was buried and forgotten under layers of dirt, and said, "I only know that it doesn't make a difference whether they stay or leave."

"OK, I'll tell you. They haven't left because they still have hope, and they are determined to achieve what they came for. I don't think they will budge. It would take superpowers to make them. Although, you know, today they might actually decide to leave. Guess why."

I looked up for the first time since we began our walk and found that we were standing at the entrance of Qasr al-Nil Bridge.

Galal continued: "Because they will run off when they wake up and see your despair-inducing face, Nadia. Your face is a picture of bleakness. Your low spirits will empty out the square. So, my love, I suggest you take yourself for a long walk outside the square, for an hour or two or ten; see what your conscience tells you. This is to protect the revolution, Nadia."

I looked at him in disbelief. "Are you throwing me out, Galal?"

He laughed. "No, my dear, I'm just trying to save our morale. I don't want the protestors to wake up to this long face."

"Morale? Whatever, Galal. You know I'm right and just don't want to admit it."

As he walked away, he called back, "OK, Nadia. Just go for a walk and come back when you're in a better mood. Bye."

I found myself alone on the bridge. I thought of following Galal, but I looked toward the square and decided there was indeed no point. So I turned and walked along the corniche. I would go home to see my father if I got tired.

I was still looking at the ground as I walked, mulling over my theory. We couldn't see anything through. We were no good at finishing things. We created momentum but faltered at the end. It really applied to everything. We made good films with naive endings, love stories that were brilliantly romantic but ended in unnecessary drama and complications. As a generation, we sucked at finishing things.

I was startled out of my thoughts by the noise of a protest march behind me. They had started early that day. I automatically stood aside and looked over at them. Large numbers filled the corniche as far as I could see. From where I stood, they seemed like the contents of a giant bag of variously colored beans, strewn all along this stretch of the corniche. Among them were recognizable uniforms: one group dressed in the black gowns of lawyers, another in the white coats of medical doctors. It was like a scene from a 1960s operetta: the extras representing the different sectors of society, surrounded by "the promising youth." The only difference was that this was not state propaganda, but its opposite. I stood on the sidewalk farthest from the Nile and watched them pass. I didn't know where they were heading, but I took a few steps, and then joined them, my thin voice repeating their chants.

The march was heading toward the center for false news: Maspero, the state television building. I started imagining the battle that would ensue. The numbers were amazing. These wild beasts—the protestors—were surely going to break into the building and fight. With these numbers, we would certainly win and occupy the building. Then it would have been a real revolution. The protest extended for a few kilometers on either side of the building. The soldiers on their tanks were getting nervous; officers talked urgently into their radios. They seemed scared, and that was a good sign: they had recognized our obvious advantage.

Protestors on the front lines started talking to the military personnel. "Hey, buddy, good morning," I overheard someone say to a young-looking soldier, who only smiled and looked away. I felt my blood rise. "Buddy"? And "good morning"? How was that the attitude of a revolutionary? Why weren't we breaking into this building that everyone agreed was a locus of oppression and corruption? Only later would I understand that there was an implicit agreement to never force entry anywhere. People kept arriving at targets and just standing there. Maybe out of fear. Maybe to preserve the principle of nonviolence. Maybe out of some presumptive trust in the military or respect for public property, which time and time again would be put above the people and their lives.

And so, even at that moment of overwhelming advantage, the protestors refused to force their way in. When I asked someone why we weren't at least going to the square instead, he replied with confidence, "The square is already full. They will fear us more if we stand here. This is a very important location. You're too young to understand."

I nodded in genuine agreement. "You're right. I really don't understand anything at all."

I ended up standing there for about eight hours, moving between the shade of a tree across the street and the front line by the barbed wire. I tried to read the expressions on the officers' faces, and when everything persisted in making no sense, I went back to the tree.

Finally I got bored and decided to go home to check on my father. I called and found him in an edgy mood.

"Listen," he said, "I'm going to get dressed and go out."

"What's the rush? Wait, I'll come get you."

"No, no, stay where you are. Aren't you at the square?"

"No, I'm by Maspero. Don't go to the square. Meet me in Talaat Harb. I'll be at Groppi in half an hour."

I ended the call and started walking. It was impossible to find a taxi, so I walked all the way to Talaat Harb Square. The sun was setting, and numbers were picking up. So was my heartbeat as I stood outside Groppi. I saw my father crossing the street, and at the same moment I heard a gunshot. I ran toward him. He was looking around, trying to determine where the noise had come from. I took his arm and pulled him quickly toward the sidewalk. Before we had time to say anything, a man came running at a mad speed, heading toward Tahrir Square and screaming, "He stepped down! He stepped down!" We exchanged looks of incomprehension. Who had stepped down? We headed toward Groppi, and found people there hugging each other and talking frantically. There had been a short statement from the former chief of intelligence and newly appointed vice president. The regime had fallen. The president had handed over his authority to the armed forces. I jumped up and down. I turned to my father to hug him and saw him standing at the door, far from me. He was smiling in relief. His face faded, then disappeared.

33

I BROUGHT OUT ALL THE cleaning tools from the wooden cupboard under the sink: the disinfectants, yellow dusters, floor cleaner, upholstery powder, bleach for the toilet, and glass cleaner. I emptied all the small trash cans into one big garbage bag. When I was young, my mother used to always give me the chore of changing the trash cans. I used to do it grudgingly. I took the full bag outside and put clean bags in all the cans. I lined up the cleaning products neatly at the kitchen threshold and prepared myself for the task ahead by lighting the first cigarette.

Silence was reigning once more between Ali and me. For a while, there had been nothing to say. He was feeling down and didn't leave his house. Did he not want to see me? I couldn't tell. I went about my days mechanically. Nothing mattered really, not then and not ever. Then he reappeared, briefly. I told him that I was fed up, that I wanted to go somewhere far away. He didn't want me to go. "Do what you want, Nadia, just don't leave me." I stared at the ceiling of the room. In truth, I didn't want to go yet—not if he still wanted me beside him. I combed his long hair, and with a kiss sent him off to work. He wanted the sacred doorstep hug to last forever. So we stayed together, united by our misery and by the doorstep hug, which was the only thing that mattered.

I put some wood-cleaning powder on the yellow cloth and sat on the floor. I rubbed the wood vigorously. There were so many stains. I wet the towel and squeezed the water out. I scrubbed and scrubbed until my hands hurt.

After another period of disappearance, Ali returned as he usually did. He spent an anxious night, then got out of bed early. Was it six? It was still dark outside. His movements woke me. He said that he was leaving and probably not coming back. His voice was loud, and I hate loud voices. He didn't want to be questioned. He didn't want to see the ceiling of this room ever again. Everything here suffocated him and increased his misery. I turned my back on him and went back to sleep, only waking when the door slammed shut. Hours later I woke up properly to realize it wasn't a bad dream. He had left and wasn't coming back. I felt angry and decided that I would tell him it really was over, that I no longer cared about him, and that I blamed him for all the floods in the universe, all the earthquakes, volcanoes, and unfinished revolutions, for all the sins of the world and all the troubles of all lovers. I sat unmoving for hours, barely breathing. This was yet another separation. It was just me and the ceiling now.

*

The cleaning was unending. The apartment was steeped in filth. The toilet couldn't be cleaned using normal methods, so I put large quantities of disinfectant on a cleaning towel and added some kerosene—I thought of using acid but was worried it would burn my hand—and pushed my arm up to my elbow into the toilet bowl. I scrubbed at the dirt that lurked in hidden places. The corners were dark yellow, as if they hadn't seen soap or water in months. I cleaned and cleaned—I had never seen the place so filthy. My fingers hurt but I continued to scrub. The smell turned my stomach but I pinched my nose with my other hand and persisted.

Days passed after Ali left. Long, suffocating days. I found it difficult to breathe. I couldn't do much beyond staring at the ceiling. My body was dug into the sofa, my limbs rigid from lying there. Ali's things were still in their usual places: his clothes neatly folded on the shelf allocated for him, his toothbrush in its place on the bathroom shelf, his small red hat on the bookshelf, the notes I used to leave for him still up on the fridge. Everything was in its usual place. I woke up every day to check that it was.

Then one day, I got a message: "I've missed you." He asked to see me. He was coming back to life, breathing again. I went to him. The toilet bowl had started to regain its clear whiteness, the yellow stains slowly disappearing. I hesitated a bit, but I went. Ali received me eagerly. I barely saw his face.

He immediately pulled me into a long embrace. The world stopped around us. I didn't see the room or him. I just let myself be in his embrace, the sweetest since we'd first met. I closed my arms around him, encircled his ribs, moved my hands along his back—I really was in his arms. It took me a few seconds to understand that this was the moment I had always sought, through other lives and in this one, in parallel universes, on faraway planets—this was the moment, and nothing else mattered.

Once again I found the spider in the bathroom. It ran away at an insane speed. The bathroom was full of insects. I sat on the floor, my legs extended before me, and started scrubbing with the brush. I poured disinfectant on the floor. A few drops weren't enough. I needed large amounts of disinfectant. Everything was filthy. Half the bottle was finished, the brush had gone black, and the wire scrubber was ruined. I brought out a new brush. I knew the drill when the place got so dirty, and I was well prepared. I lit my fifth cigarette and started cleaning the bathroom floor with the new brush. My clothes were dirty and wet. It was cold and I was shivering a little. The ashtray was next to me. I didn't want to dirty the floor further with my cigarette ash.

The last time I saw Ali he didn't sleep. I talked and talked and talked, fearing the return of the silence between us. He hadn't said a word in days. Then, early one morning, he called and said calmly that our story was over. It wasn't ever a story. A miserable one? Maybe. He insisted that it wasn't love, and that whatever it was, it really was over. There was no going back. I listened without comment. Then I asked a few brief questions, and he repeated that this time he was leaving and not coming back. He said that I should leave too. He spoke persistently and I persisted in listening. I wanted details. I wanted him to tell me that he had never loved me, that he was never happy with me. And he said it all. Then he was done talking.

I got up quietly and went to the mirror. I looked into my reddened eyes. I was at boiling point. I felt the floor rising vertically to meet me. I sat down and rubbed my head. Then I stood up and went over to the shelves. I took his clothes, found the bag he had left behind, and stuffed his clothes into it. I went to the fridge, took off all the notes, folded them, and stuck them in the bag's outer pocket. I went to the bathroom for his toothbrush. Then I got his beautiful hat. I was going to miss that hat. When everything was in the bag, I put the bag by the front door and lay down beside it. The floor was cold—cold and dirty. I saw that I still had a long day of cleaning ahead. I don't know how many hours I lay like that—facing Ali's bag, my cheek stuck to the floor. I felt myself sink into the wooden floor. My arms extended motionless beside me. Only then did I recognize it as the moment of the ending. I fell asleep.

34

The sun doesn't enter the small apartment in the morning. There's a large window that takes up the entire width of a wall, but its thick glass never sees direct sunlight. On the other side of the glass there are buildings, some built in the eighties and some much older. And there's the garden of an embassy that has been there for years. I never paid attention to the colors of the flag raised in its yard.

The sky is as pale as my father's face on that day long ago, a disturbing grayish white and blue, by turns terrifying and reassuringly calm. I can still see the colors that passed over my father's face in those few moments. Nine years have gone by since I stood staring at him as he lay in the hospital's mortuary fridge, terrifying and familiar, resentful of death, finally free of the world's unending troubles, and angry about the unfinished revolutions he would miss.

I haven't reached thirty yet. My father left when I was barely twenty-one, a few months after Zayn. Baba, I have done so much in your name: countless marches in the streets of Cairo, demonstrations in which I raised my thin voice in chants, unadulterated joy at the fall of a corrupt regime, nights spent sleeping on the ground in the square. I even broke my heart once or twice in your name. You didn't see me and you missed the incomplete miracles that were like messages of half-prophets. You had gone to a place of peace and comfort, nine years before.

I spent innumerable hours in my kitchen, knowing full well you weren't coming. I still served your favorite dishes and sat before them talking to you about revolutions and sit-ins and successive defeats. I heard your voice every step of the way. Every time I was confused, I heard your loud, reassuring laughter. I kept seeing you. I saw you looking at me through the flimsy cloth of the burial shroud. I saw you pound your hands on the walls of the narrow tomb, brush aside the dead bones that surrounded you, and come out to console me after each new departure. You came back to sit with me at the metal table in our favorite restaurant, to be silent with me, and occasionally to chide me for my recklessness and stupid choices. You were always there, always and everywhere, holding my hand and pulling me into a hug that lasted beyond the end of the world.

Nine slow, cruel years have passed. And ten years since Zayn. When I lost Zayn, you were there to make sure that I was still breathing and my heart was still beating. But no one was there to watch over what I became when you left.

The color of the sky doesn't change much in the evening; it only becomes darker and sadder. So many lights glow behind the big window. Faraway lights that appear and disappear. From behind the window they look enticing, but if you look closely, you see them for what they are: billboards for cooking oils, for tourist resorts promising a better life. Which is why it's always best to look from a distance.

I get up from the sofa that has been my refuge for nine years. I've only ever wanted to leave it when the loud call of demonstrations summoned me. I went and imagined you with me, holding my hand. I clung to you as you tried, from your grave, to protect me, but failed. The window is behind the sofa so I don't have to face the sky every day and think of your face. There's the customary background noise of the TV. I wake up to find marks on my side or my stomach, and discover that the remote control was stuck to my skin as I slept. I wonder why I don't turn off the TV before I sleep.

The same morning headache, the same morning moroseness. It takes me at least two hours to get up and brush my teeth. I count the vitamin pills that I've collected from every country I've ever visited: one for hair loss, one for memory and focus, and the magic one for energy. I swallow them all, together with two capsules for the headache, and put fresh coffee in the machine. Only when the aroma of the coffee mixing with water reaches me do I start to reluctantly wake up to the world.

I don't work much any more. A few years ago I managed to save enough money and pull a few tricks to get an arrangement for the least possible working hours. It's not laziness. It's just that I've discovered my inability to stay committed to anything. When did I become like this? Was it when you died, Baba? I think I made up my mind as I said my last goodbye to you at the entrance of the narrow tomb: never again will I invest my feelings in living beings. That was the angry vow I made to you. I blamed you for deceiving me by letting me get attached to your presence when you must have known you weren't staying. I unwrapped the shroud around your head and feet and told you calmly that I wasn't angry at *you*. I was just bitter and frustrated, and was faking my calmness in order not to upset you further. I knew you didn't like change. Moving to that small tomb was certain to make you anxious, at least until you got used to your new companions. I didn't want to make things more difficult for you, so before I climbed the ladder that led out of the dusty grave I told you that I wasn't angry, just too clever to make the same mistake again. No one and nothing will ever again become the center of my life. I won't sign any contracts, and won't make anything indispensable to me. That was my vow of self-protection.

Everything comes to an end, Father, even you.

I wake up the same as I do every day, bored and peaceful. I open my laptop and stare at the email that has been waiting for a month. It's finally time. I print it out and place the paper on top of my large suitcase that's standing by the door. On that last day, having diligently smoked my seventh cigarette, I put it out, pick up my keychain, and detach the key of my small apartment. I get dressed, lift the suitcase, and step outside. In the elevator, I am met by the neighbor who gives me the same suspicious smile he's been treating me to since I started living here nine years ago. I look down and stare at my purple shoes. Seconds before the elevator reaches the ground floor, I say without looking at him, "I work as a translator. I translate books. I'm moving out today. Take care." He looks at me in surprise, shakes his head vigorously, and says, "You will be missed, Miss Nadia."

I get out of the elevator, hand the key to the building's caretaker, and take a taxi to the airport. Umm Kulthum sings out of the car radio.

You are closer to me than myself
Whether you are here or far away

I check my passport and the printout of the ticket that will take me to Radwa, and then I sit back and glue my face to the window. I watch the world outside go by. Maybe one day I will return and start again.

Selected Hoopoe Titles

Whitefly
by Abdelilah Hamdouchi, translated by Jonathan Smolin

The Final Bet
by Abdelilah Hamdouchi, translated by Jonathan Smolin

A Beautiful White Cat Walks with Me
by Youssef Fadel, translated by Alexander E. Elinson

*

hoopoe is an imprint for engaged, open-minded readers hungry for outstanding fiction that challenges headlines, re-imagines histories, and celebrates original storytelling. Through elegant paperback and digital editions, **hoopoe** champions bold, contemporary writers from across the Middle East alongside some of the finest, groundbreaking authors of earlier generations.

At hoopoefiction.com, curious and adventurous readers from around the world will find new writing, interviews, and criticism from our authors, translators, and editors.